2015

I DARE YOU TO TRY IT

ELIE JEROME

All rights reserved.

Copyright © 2015 by Elie Jerome.

Library of Congress Control Number: 2015911499

Elie Jerome, Brooklyn New York

ISBN:	Softcover	978-0-9965510-0-7
ISBN:	eBook	978-0-9965510-2-1

This is a work of fiction. The events and characters portrayed are imaginary. Their resemblance, if any, to real-life counterparts is entirely coincidental.

No part of this book may be reproduced or transmitted in any form or by any means, electronic or mechanical, including photocopying, recording, or by any information storage and retrieval system, without permission in writing from the copyright owner.

To order additional copies of this book go to:
www.amazon.com

I DARE YOU TO TRY IT

This book is dedicated to my cousin, James Annastal, (1978-2004). He was one of the best writers I have ever known. Gone but never forgotten.

Acknowledgement

I am speechless and more than thankful to the Almighty God who grants me life, health, knowledge and a creative mind to write this story.

I thank my wife, Isabelle Devilme Jerome, for her love and constructive comments about the story. *"You're my Kamikaz."*

A special thanks from the bottom of my heart to Basiliki Thompson, the best editor I have ever worked with. Thanks also to Professor Yasmine Alwan and Professor Parker Pracjek at Metropolitan College of New York (MCNY), Clairsine Plaisir, Kimberly Jean, Josephine Farella and Mikelson Blemont for their hard work in editing the book.

I have no words to express my gratitude to LeeAnn King-Bushey, Cathy and Carrie Brzezinski. Their love and appreciation go beyond measure. I will be forever grateful to them.

I have used the names of some family members and friends in this book to show my gratefulness for their unceasing encouragement and support. And I hope to use more names in future scriptures because the list of my benefactors is very long.

In addition, I wish to express my sincere thankfulness to all staff members in Division of Cardiology, administration building at Maimonides Medical Center for their love, caring, and availability to participate in certain surveys. *"They are so shoopsss."*

And from the bottom of my heart, I thank all of you who bought the book.

Gratitude to all of you who directly or indirectly, make my dream comes true.

JUNE 1, 2012

At 7:40 p.m., the gentleman wore his black suit on his way to his second job. It was his first time working on a Friday night as bouncer for *Team Undercover*. He had to cover for a security guard who went on vacation. His only regret was that he would not be able to watch *Spartacus,* his favorite TV show. He took the 3 train heading to the Bronx. He was playing a brick game on his Blackberry, unaware of what was about to happen that night.

Calm as usual, he got off at Atlantic Avenue and transferred to the B train for West 4th Street. Around 8:30 p.m., the gentleman reached his destination: *The Flow,* a bar and restaurant on 90 West 3rd Street. The gentleman met

Carl Henry, the manager of *The Flow* who suggested to him that he take a walk and come back one hour later. He stepped out of the bar and went to the McDonald's on West 3rd Street where he ordered a hamburger and a smoothie.

At 9:25 p.m., he left the fast food restaurant and headed back to *The Flow* where he received instructions and equipment from Carl to start at 9:30 p.m. He had to work with another security guard who came in at 9:45 p.m.

The Flow had two floors: the first floor was a restaurant from 11:00 a.m. until 10:00 p.m. when it turned into a lounge for cocktails and the second floor was a dancing room opened from 10:00 p.m. to 4:00 a.m. *The Flow* had all glass doors and an old rustic staircase that led to the second floor, where large windows looked out onto West 3rd Street. It contained a bar with some bar stools. Attached to the cement walls were two big flat screen TV's that played sports games until 11:30 p.m. Every Friday, a large crowd composed mostly of college students gathered at the lounge to enjoy its affordable drinks.

"Good evening, ID please?" the gentleman asked like he was a programmed robot. After inspecting information on each ID card, he thanked, welcomed, and opened the door for the customers. He paid attention to every single detail in the place because he wanted to make sure he provided his best service.

Antoine Perez, the other bouncer arrived at 9:55 p.m. He was five feet nine inches tall, muscular, good-looking with a clean haircut and dark brown eyes, and friendly. He wore a black suit with a black t-shirt. Perez made a quick introduction of himself to the gentleman. He explained everything to the gentleman about the bar and its customers and helped his new colleague to set up the security equipment.

Activities were slow that night due to a little rain earlier. The DJ was barely playing any good music. Many customers left *The Flow* to go to other bars. Carl ended up shutting down the second floor. However, the few customers who stayed were having a good time. They were talking about work, relationships, politics, and many other subjects. There was also a nerdy college kid trying to talk to every woman. He was out of his league and comical to watch.

Perez stood beside the gentleman in front of the doors and observed his attitude. He glanced at him many times and wondered why his co-worker remained quiet. Finally he asked, "Why don't you say anything to any girl?"

The gentleman chuckled and replied, "I'm like that, quiet at work."

"Relax! No stress man. That's how we do it here."

Even though Perez worked for over three years at *The Flow* and nothing bad happened, he knew he had an unprofessional attitude. For him, looking for friendship that led to sex showed skills of a macho man. Thus, he wanted the gentleman to have that same mindset. As the night went on, the gentleman stood like an English guard in front of the doors and limited his conversation. Meanwhile, Perez, who worked every day at the bar, was enjoying cigarettes with customers.

As time passed, many ladies were wandering in the streets — some alone and others accompanied by their friends. The gentleman flashed a glance at his watch almost every fifteen minutes; he could not wait until 4:30 a.m. to go home.

Around 2:15 a.m., a lady who appeared to be in her early twenties walked by *The Flow*. She looked attractive and was alone. She wore a green mini skirt and an off-white blouse. The lady was curvy and carried a green purse over her shoulder. She looked at the two good-looking bouncers, smiled at them, and continued to walk.

Perez glared after the lady for few seconds, and then he nudged his co-worker, blew a whistle, and commented, "Damn! Shorty looks good, man."

The gentleman acknowledged his comment and nodded, "Yeah man, she does."

They glared at her ass as she was strutting away. Half way down the block, the lady turned back and smiled once again at the bouncers. Perez rubbed his chin and could not resist her charm anymore.

"Yo! I'll be right back, gonna holla at that chick," he said before he followed the lady.

The gentleman shook his head, smiled, and kept doing his job.

Half way down the block, Perez realized the lady was too far ahead. He came back to his post and said, "She's interested, man."

"Yeah, so why'd you come back alone?" the gentleman mocked.

"I ain't walking two blocks down to talk to that bitch. Are you crazy?"

The gentleman smiled at him and focused on his job. Five minutes later, the lady came to the bouncers and asked, "Who wanna drive me home?"

Perez could not wait for that moment. With his right hand dipped into his pocket, he asked her, "Where do you live?"

"Brooklyn," she answered.

Perez stared at the lady and started his speech with a flirting smile, "You're a beautiful lady. I won't mind taking you home."

"Don't think I'm gonna have sex with you for a ride," she snapped.

"Who said anything about sex? And I don't think it's a bad idea to have sex with such a pretty lady like you. My name is Perez. What's your name?"

The lady looked at him, shook her head, and answered, "Tatyana."

Perez took four steps toward Tatyana, shook her right hand and said, "Nice to meet you Tatyana. Do you have a cigarette?"

Asking for cigarette or a lighter is a simple request that could lead to a long conversation. Smoking means we have the same connection — we could share words, emotions, and desire. Obviously, nobody has to wonder why residents in big cities buy so many cigarettes. Unfortunately for Perez, it didn't work out well for him this time.

"No, I don't. I'm sorry, I don't smoke," Tatyana answered with a firm tone of voice.

The gentleman remained quiet and stood straight by the doors as three women walked by; one in her mid-twenties and two who appeared to be in their fifties. They were on their way home from another bar. From the smiles on their faces, anyone could tell they were having a great time together.

Five feet after they passed *The Flow,* the youngest woman stopped, turned her head back, and said to the gentleman, "Can you hug and kiss her for me please? She's my mom. She's visiting New York City. It's her first time."

The gentleman glared at her for a couple of seconds. This could not be real; her beauty and confidence amazed him. She wore a strapless, off white short dress with yellow shoes and a heart's medallion on her neck suspended just at the exposed top of her breasts. Her long, natural, black hair fell along the left side of her face. She held a gold purse in her left hand and wore a nice gold bracelet on her right wrist. With her five feet seven inch frame accentuated by her heels, she looked gorgeous with her gold sparkly fingernails.

The two other women stared at the gentleman and hoped he did not deny her simple request. He smiled at the youngest woman and said, "Of course, no problem." The gentleman did not want to refuse a favor to a woman who could have been his own mother.

The mother of the youngest woman moved toward the gentleman with a smile and happiness of a child who was about to receive a Christmas gift. He drew her into his arms and she said, "He smells so good."

The satisfaction of the mother following that hug aroused curiosity in all the other women present at the scene. Smart people do not think twice when great opportunity is presented. Suddenly, the other older woman walked toward him and said, "Let me have a hug as well."

The gentleman opened his arms and hugged her. She exclaimed, "Oh my God, you smell soooo gooood!"

"Oh yes, he does. I like his cologne," added the mother of the youngest woman.

Perez and Tatyana stopped their conversation and paid attention to the comedy that would turn into an unbelievable night. The youngest woman among the three motioned toward the gentleman with a confidence from nowhere and said, "Since I asked for a hug and kiss and you already gave the hugs, let me have the kiss then."

"Where do you want it?"

With no hesitation the woman put her finger to her lips to point out the destination of the kiss. The gentleman wondered if he was dreaming. Before he could pinch himself, or even note his hesitation and desire, he was already kissing the beautiful young stranger.

Perez and Tatyana glanced at each other and then stared at that unexpected exchange of feeling. They were shocked. The two other women laughed and clapped their hands together like it was a wedding. The youngest woman went deep into that kiss. It seemed she had been waiting for a moment like that for so long. A few seconds after, the bouncer and the young princess stopped kissing and smiled at each other.

"Wow, wow, wow," was the only word that Tatyana could pronounce at that moment.

Tatyana stood with her hands on her thick hips and mouth half opened. She could taste the sweetness of that kiss. Her eyes told how much she would love to live such a moment in her life. Her heart was pounding so loud that no one had to be close to hear it. What a weird sensation felt by Tatyana, like the gentleman was her boyfriend. She licked and bit the bottom of her lip like she was the one who received that kiss or maybe she wished to receive one like that. Tatyana did not have that much courage to ask for one as well and regretfully said, "Unbelievable!"

"They are so cute," added the mother of the youngest woman.

The youngest woman satisfied, compressed her lips, and looked at the bouncer. With her eyes semi-closed, she smiled at him and said, "Thank you."

Perez realized that his co-worker made a big mistake. So he ran to the gentleman and said, "Are you crazy? You just did that in front of the camera. Yo man! They will fire you. Every morning they review the camera from the prior night. You should have gone in the corner. I've been here for many years and I have never done that."

"I am sorry. I didn't mean to cause you any trouble," the youngest woman said to the gentleman.

One thing was sure — the youngest woman was not worried because she saw the calmness of the gentleman through his eyes. Only a real man and a leader could bring such comfort when panic arose.

The gentleman smiled at her and replied, "Don't worry. It's okay. Everything will be fine."

Some sweet moments come once in lifetime; one must seizes them and enjoy them. That kiss turned into a feeling that penetrated her body, ran into her blood, and transformed into a sensation that travelled to her brain. It invaded her heart and made her so weak that she could not stand up anymore. She went to sit down on the stairs of another building next to *The Flow*. She was afraid to look the bouncer straight into his eyes, but he held her captive with his eyes and his lips.

Love is strong and violent when tasted in its fullness. It brings strength to stand against any adversity. Less than one minute was enough to convince the gentleman to not give a hoot about the job and ask for a second kiss.

"Let's do it one more time."

"No, No. That's enough," the youngest woman replied.

She managed to stay still, but deep inside she was fighting with a feeling of guilt and a strong desire to do it one more time. No one understood that answer from the youngest woman. The kiss was wonderful, but the eyes of the gentleman were killing her heart softly. He knew how to communicate with his eyes. God blessed him with brown eyes circled by a blue and yellow line as if he wore contacts.

The mother of the youngest woman took her daughter's left arm and said, "Come, come." She paused and then insisted, "Give him a second kiss."

People may say many negative things about love, but it will remain the most beautiful sensation and strongest emotion ever felt. Love opens the sky, makes the sun shine at midnight, stops time, and cures all wounds. Love is paradise and love is God.

It was like in a movie where everyone knew his or her roles. The street was quiet. Perez and Tatyana did not say a word. It seemed like time had stopped and no noise could be heard, like there was no sin on earth. A soft breeze blew in the street and carried a smell of peace and harmony.

Perez pulled his co-worker over to the corner of the building and away from the camera as the youngest lady moved toward the gentleman for another kiss. They exchanged love and desire without pride, hesitation, or fear. Love is so simple it does not need years to be felt. It is so sweet it can transform a lion into a lamb.

The gentleman held the youngest woman's hips, smiled at her, and then he looked at her eyes for a couple of seconds like he was hypnotizing her. She trembled, sank, and she melted in his arms. What a sublime moment. It reminded him of the moment when Neo in Matrix Reloaded had to kiss Persephone for the key. However, this kiss represented not only the key for a possible friendship, but it also brought love back to the gentleman's heart.

They kissed for almost two minutes. That kiss could be considered as the kiss of the century. The youngest woman satisfied more than ever, smiled, and walked toward her house. Her mother and the other woman followed her. Only love can make one weak in one kiss and strong after the next kiss.

The gentleman followed the beautiful stranger and asked her, "May I have your number, please?"

"I am sorry. I can't give it to you," she replied.

"You asked me for a hug and kiss for your mother, I gave it to her and her friend. Don't disappear like that. I want to see you again."

"Don't worry. You will see me often because I always take this path to go to my house and the manager of *The Flow* is my friend."

"Can I have an email or business card or something else?" the gentleman insisted.

"I live in the area. You have seven days to find me," the youngest lady challenged him and continued to head toward her house.

He'd gone from Matrix to James Bond. Only his heart could help him find the youngest woman in that short period because he worked as a bouncer only on Friday and Saturday night. The gentleman shook his head and could not believe that she did not give him her phone number, but instead gave him such a difficult mission.

The mother's friend of the youngest woman came to the gentleman. She understood that mission was impossible for him, so she offered some hints. "I am Anna. Her mother is Carlette and her name is Laurie Lugbowskovsky. Remember her name. Laurie Lugbowskovsky, Laurie Lugbowskovsky. That's a name you should never forget. She works for *Pelito & Co,* an investment bank on Wall Street."

The mother of the youngest woman, Carlette Lugbowskovsky, motioned toward the gentleman and hugged him. Then she thanked him, held his face, and said, "She goes to *Butterfly* every Friday. It's another bar down the block. She lives at 634 Thompson Street."

Both Anna and Carlette did their best to help the bouncer find the youngest woman. However, he could not remember such a name because his body was on earth and his mind on Venus. The gentleman felt like a boxer who

I Dare You To Try It   21

was knocked out and could remember nothing. Anna and Carlette left and followed Laurie. The gentleman regained his post and acted like nothing happened.

"Oh yeah, that's the way you do it guys, huh?" Tatyana demanded.

Perez wanted to get lucky as well and hoped that Tatyana would make the same request as the youngest woman did. He tried to play innocent and pleaded, "We do talk to women, but nothing like that happened before."

Tatyana kept her eyes on the gentleman as if Perez did not exist for her anymore. A strong desire to taste the gentleman's lips came over her right away. She stood less than five feet away from him, but she did not know how to request a kiss from him. She feared rejection and her intuition told her that the gentleman would not kiss her after tasting the lips of that beautiful young woman. Tatyana was consumed by the regret of not being the lucky one while she was the first who came and talked to the bouncers. "That's why you never say a word. You are quiet and smart. You have your special way to catch a female."

The gentleman smiled at Tatyana, acknowledging in his mind that her comment was true.

A taxi came and Tatyana waved her hand to stop it. Perez asked her to keep him company for a little bit. He also told her he would drop her off wherever she wanted. She declined his offer with a head movement. Perez opened the door of the cab for Tatyana, trying to think of any magic words to convince her. However, she did not take her eyes off of the gentleman and hoped that he would ask her to stay for a few more minutes. Perez whispered words to her, but none of them seemed to penetrate her ears.

The taxi driver honked. Tatyana desperate, sighed, and got into the car. She told the taxi driver her destination and left the place without even saying one word to Perez.

"You should follow them man. That's how you can fuck them bro. Those white chicks are like that. They get drunk and then they fuck with whoever pleases their eyes," Perez suggested after regaining his post by the doors beside the gentleman.

"I know man."

"You would have a good time man. That bitch is hot. Damn! They like you bro and you would fuck the mother also man, or all three. I wish it was me bro. I'm telling you man," Perez continued with an ironic smile.

Perez underestimated the gentleman. He might have a lot more experience in security than his co-worker, but not in women. Silence and a smile are the most effective tools to show innocence and hide one's capabilities. The Bible says answer the fool with wisdom, and a smile was the best answer that the gentleman could give to Perez.

Although Perez's assessment sounded foolish and crazy, he was right. The gentleman should have chased them because it was the perfect moment to strike. Good time at a restaurant with family, a couple of drinks, felt tipsy, kisses on the way home, and happiness was all over the place. The youngest woman was turned on and the mother ready to grant permission to the gentleman who could be covered by Perez during his absence. Crazy things may happen everywhere, but not like they do in New York City. Welcome to the Big Apple.

Perez went inside the bar to make sure that everything was fine with the customers, but most of all if anybody else had been watching the epic scene. The gentleman thought about what Perez had just told him. After a long night standing and trying to maintain order within a place full with people who drank and smoked, one deserves acknowledgement. As a single man, there could be no better reward for a bouncer than having a woman who wanted to spend the rest of the night with him in her bed or somewhere else. The gentleman stared blank over the street and replayed in his mind the amazing moment he'd just had.

Certain things happen once in a lifetime. When opportunity comes, one should acknowledge it and take advantage of it. Like in a game, if you score once, you can score many times. It doesn't matter the duration, how and where a man has sex with a woman as long as it is done safely. Once a woman gives the green light to a man, he should speed up. The first time is what matters.

Perez returned quickly and demanded, "Are you going after them or not?"

Tick tock, tick tock, tick tock, the gentleman had only a few seconds to make up his mind. He was not under pressure from Perez; he had to decide between his mind and his heart. That kiss touched the deepest part of his heart. He was no longer thinking about physical pleasure, but was already dreaming about living life in love with the youngest woman.

It is always interesting to see how quickly the human mind works to make decisions between different options and how a simple moment can change one's life forever. These kinds of choices forge mankind's destiny.

"No man, don't worry," the gentleman answered.

"Are you sure bro?"

"Yeah man."

Perez looked at the gentleman like something was wrong with him. He remained silent because he did not understand the reaction of his co-worker. Perez thought maybe the gentleman was gay, but he did not dare to ask him question about his sexual preference.

Around 2:50 a.m., customers started leaving *The Flow*. The gentleman went inside to make sure everything was fine and seized that opportunity to take a walk and clear his mind. One hour later, all the customers had left the bar. The waitresses made their reports to Carl, and then they gave him the money they collected for the night, and cleaned the rooms.

The bouncers took three shots of Vodka and Tequila after closing the doors. They discussed how long they had been working for *Team Undercover*. Work was done, so they both left *The Flow* at 4:30 a.m. They headed toward the D train station. Perez stopped by a green Mitsubishi

Limited 2000 and said, "That's my car. Where do you live?"

"In Brooklyn."

"Oh man. I'm from the Bronx. I wish I could drop you off."

"Don't worry man. I'll take the train. Thanks for your help."

"Good night bro. I hope tomorrow nobody notices what happened tonight."

"Thanks bro. I hope so too. It was a pleasure working with you tonight. See you later man," the gentleman said.

Perez started his car and drove off. The gentleman continued his walk and took the train toward home. He felt exhausted after such a long day — from 9:00 a.m. on Friday to 4:30 a.m. the next day. The gentleman was thinking about one thing, his bed. He reached home by 5:50 a.m., opened the door, took off his clothes, took a quick shower then went straight to bed after the exhausting day. They say if one succeeds in New York City, one can succeed anywhere. This city requires sacrifice and determination to reach one's goals.

JUNE 2, 2012

Around 10:30 a.m., the gentleman woke up with his mind racing with thoughts of what happened between him and the youngest woman. Yet, he shoved away the idea of thinking about the scene because he did not sleep enough. He put his pillow over his head and then rolled back and forth on his bed to get back to sleep. But it did not work.

It was strange because she was not the first female who'd kissed him. Sometimes, he did have sex with other female customers after he finished his security guard duties. But that kiss was completely different from what he used to receive. The youngest woman kissed him with love while other women kissed him because they were looking for extra fun.

The gentleman thought a lot that Saturday morning. He was in a dilemma. He did not know if he should consider the youngest woman like the other women he used to be with after work or like the woman he'd wished to meet one day. So he had to put on his James Bond suit to find the best answers and complete the mission. He lay on his back, both hands behind his head with eyes to the ceiling, and questioned himself. He reviewed the whole scene in his mind to create a profile of the youngest woman.

After a couple of minutes, the gentleman found some key answers. He realized the youngest woman was family-oriented because she was with her mother and a friend of her mother. The way the youngest woman talked and the capabilities of Anna and Carlette to give him key information about the youngest woman, allowed him to understand they were tipsy, but not drunk. Between *Butterfly* and *The Flow,* there were two nightclubs, five restaurants, and four bars with bouncers standing in front of each. But the gentleman was the lucky one to receive that kiss. Thus, he accepted the venture.

The gentleman left his bed around 11:45 a.m. and took a shower. His bedroom was decorated with posters of some of the greatest soccer and basketball players. There was a big mirror on the left side of his bed next to a closet and a drawer that contained his underwear and his t-shirts. The gentleman put his watches, cologne, and hair brush on top of the drawer. His bedroom looked cleaned and well organized.

After the shower, he headed to the kitchen and ate eggs, bread, and a banana, and drank a cup of orange juice. Once he finished his breakfast, he went to the living room, sat down on the sofa, and turned on the TV to watch a Spanish soccer game. The gentleman became impatient and could not wait for 8:00 p.m. to leave his house in pursuit of the beautiful stranger. His intuition told him she was special.

Around the same time, Carlette and Anna were having their breakfast in the kitchen, talking about the night they'd experienced in New York City.

"What a great night we had last night," Anna said.

"I had a lot of fun," Carlette replied.

"Food was good at the restaurant and the wine was perfect. It has been a while since I drank like that," Anna confessed.

"I really enjoyed dancing at *Butterfly*. I felt young again. I was so happy."

"Oh! And by the way, what do you think about that bouncer we met at the end?" Anna asked.

"Oh my gosh, that was unexpected. He was so nice to us."

"He is tall, sexy, and smelled good. He treated us well and was very interesting."

Both Anna and Carlette desired to say something about the kiss, but none of them had the courage to bring that subject up. Laurie was listening to the conversation between her mother and Anna. She came in the kitchen, kissed them, and said,

"He kissed me."

"I remember you were the one who asked for it," Carlette said.

"That's true. To be honest, it was great and the second kiss made me feel like I was in heaven," Laurie said with a big smile.

"Wow, we saw that. I thought it was a wedding," Anna added.

"I wish I could've shared that kiss with you, but you're just too old for that," Laurie said ironically. They all laughed out loud. She grabbed a slice of toast and some apple juice and sat down at the kitchen table with them.

Definitely the end of last night was the best moment of the entire day for Anna, Carlette, and Laurie. One thing is certain, anyone who visits New York City experiences at least one unexpected moment that will stay as a memory forever.

They enjoyed the breakfast made by Anna. Five minutes later, Carlette said to her daughter,

"You're smart, girl. You asked hugs for us and a kiss for yourself."

"I am sorry to be that selfish. You told me you lived love when daddy was alive. Anna has a husband who kisses her every day. But me, I am like Cinderella."

In front of such truth, Carlette just looked at her daughter, smiled, and said, "That's true love. And I pray you to find the man you deserve."

"I hope he finds you soon," Anna added.

"Thanks," Laurie added with a wry smile.

They finished their breakfast around 12:40 a.m. Carlette did the dishes and cleaned the kitchen and Anna took care of the bedrooms. Laurie straightened up the living room and cleaned the bathroom.

Around 2:30 p.m., they left their apartment, went to a restaurant for lunch, and then they went shopping on 34th Street. For any visitor of any city, shopping is always an important piece that makes a vacation or a trip special.

Something was guiding the gentleman's mind. He left his house around 5:30 p.m. instead of 8:00 p.m. He felt he needed time to find the youngest woman. The gentleman also knew that this Saturday was his last chance to see her once again before the deadline she'd given him.

The gentleman got off the D train on West 4th Street at 6:30pm. He walked toward *The Flow*. He remembered the name and street number that Carlette told him. He used the GPS on his phone to find the address. When he got there, he saw a building instead of a house with a list of all the tenants of the building at the entrance. Also, to get access to any apartment in that building, one must choose the apartment number, then press the buzzer, and wait to be buzzed in. Unfortunately, he could not remember the name of the youngest woman. The gentleman looked carefully at all names and pressed number E13 because the name for apartment E13 appeared to be the most difficult name among all. He pressed it three times, but no answer.

The gentleman went to *Washington Square Park* located two blocks away from the building. He thought maybe they could be there. It was his first time at the park. During his search, he saw many people strolling around and found a fountain in the middle of the park. His mind was too busy to contemplate the beauty of the park. He walked through the entire park. The gentleman looked around, but did not find Carlette, Anna, or the youngest woman. He felt more pressure after this try because it was getting dark.

The gentleman left the park. He was more than determined to find the youngest woman. He went into *Butterfly* to see if they were there. When he arrived, there was a security guard standing in front of the door.

"Can I come in?" The gentleman asked.

"It's ten dollars," the bouncer of *Butterfly* replied.

"I am not staying. I just want to see if my friend is inside or not."

"It doesn't matter how long you're gonna stay buddy."

"I am a security guard also. I work for *The Flow*."

"I see that, but I am sorry man. The rules are rules."

The gentleman could not believe the security guard of *Butterfly* did not let him go inside. He wanted to find the youngest woman, and time was running against him. In

United States of America, time is money and every single opportunity could come to involve money.

"Okay, give me five dollars and I will let you come in," the bouncer said.

The gentleman hesitated for a few seconds, but decided not to take the bouncer's offer and walked back toward *The Flow*. He passed *The Flow* and stopped on the corner of Thompson Street to make an observation. The gentleman saw a deli situated just in front of the building where the youngest woman likely lived.

The gentleman went inside the grocery store and asked the owner of the deli about the youngest woman. Despite all the information given by the gentleman, the owner of the deli could not recognize her, even though he claimed to know almost all the tenants in that building.

At that moment, the gentleman lost faith in his mission. He bought an energy drink and a pack of gum and left the grocery. Right after he stepped out of the store, he saw three women crossing Thompson Street. He ran and said, "Hello, good evening ladies."

The targeted women did not turn back nor stop. Therefore, the gentleman walked closer to them and snapped, "Ladies."

They were about to enter the building when the youngest among the three women, had an impression someone was addressing them. So she turned her head, saw the gentleman, and said, "Oh my gosh, it's you!"

"Yes it is," the gentleman replied.

Anna and Carlette stopped walking, turned back, and saw the gentleman. They were so happy that they ran to him and hugged him.

"You found us. That's great. How are you doing?" Anna asked in delight.

"Yes I did. I am fine. Thanks. What about you?"

"We are doing great. You always smell so good," Carlette said.

"We talked a lot about you today. You are a very nice person," Anna stated.

"Thank you so much. I have met many people before, but last night you made it very special," the gentleman confessed.

"That's so sweet of you," the youngest woman said.

"How did you find us?" Anna asked with curiosity.

He shook his head, smiled, and said, "I thought a lot about that deadline. I couldn't even sleep."

"What deadline did you have?" the youngest woman asked.

"You told me I have seven days to find you."

His answer surprised the youngest woman. So she asked, "Really? Did I tell you that?"

"Yes, you did. I remember that," Carlette confirmed.

"Well, I must congratulate you. You are quick," the youngest woman acknowledged.

"And smart," Anna added with a smile.

The gentleman explained all the steps he took to find them. Carlette, Anna, and the youngest woman listened carefully to his journey in search of the stranger. He told them how difficult it was for him to remember the name of the youngest woman. So the youngest woman made a formal introduction. She said, "I'm Laurie and the apartment number you pressed was mine."

"Nice to meet you Laurie, I am…."

Anna was more than convinced that the bouncer was the man Laurie was meant to meet. Anna had a sixth sense that recruiters in Human Resources use to select the best employees within a few minutes. She did not let him introduce himself. She said, "I think you guys were supposed to meet. It's not a coincidence."

Anna was one of the rare people who knew that the word *Luck* itself did not exist. *Luck* is a word used by people who did not take action when great opportunities were presented. They used it to describe the success of those who have acted. People like Anna use the word *Faith* to describe what others call *Luck*.

Laurie and the gentleman glanced at each other and smiled, even though they did not understand or believe what Anna just said. Carlette and Anna understood the connection between Laurie and the gentleman. So they decided to give them some time alone.

"We are tired. We're going upstairs. It was a great pleasure to meet and see you again," Carlette said.

"I hope we will see you before we leave New York. We're going back to Michigan on Monday," Anna added.

"Pleasure was mine to meet such wonderful people like you. And I wish I could spend more time with you before you leave. If I don't see you again I wish you a safe trip and pray to see you once again in New York."

Anna and Carlette hugged him and went to apartment #E13. For a few seconds, Laurie and the gentleman stared at each other, but neither said a word. During that silence, Laurie was thinking about what the bouncer had thought about last night. She did not want him to take her as an easy woman.

Meanwhile, the gentleman was admiring the beauty of Laurie in her high waist skinny black jeans with a low white tank tucked into her jeans. She wore peep toe ankle strap beige heels. Laurie looked hot with her red lipstick and her red fingernails.

Often, people look gorgeous, handsome, and beautiful at night when it is not bright. To grade the beauty of anyone in such an environment, appearance plays a key role. Although the concept of beauty is subjective, no one could deny the beauty of Laurie. The gentleman realized that all his efforts were worth his adventure.

"Do you know that you have an amazing smile?"

"Thank you."

"Where did you get it from?"

"I guess it is from my mother," Laurie said with a bright smile.

For an unknown reason, she could not look the gentleman straight in his eyes. She was nervous to make eye contact with him. He realized that, so he did his best to make her feel comfortable.

"I had a great night because of you."

"Thanks. I am happy to hear that. How is everything at *The Flow*? Did they say anything to you about what happened last night?" Laurie asked with a concerned tone.

"I haven't gone there yet. So I don't know what they're gonna say. But I am pretty sure everything will be okay."

"You are calm. And I like that."

"Thank you."

They had a good conversation together. Laurie talked about her Friday night's routine. He told her about his Friday and Saturday nights in nightclubs or restaurants. Throughout their conversation, the bouncer mentioned nothing about the kiss. He did not want to keep Laurie any longer — not because it was already 9:00 p.m., but he knew that she had to entertain her mother and Anna before they left New York.

"So I know you will have to go upstairs soon, but before you do, can I ask you one more question?"

"Go ahead."

"I don't know why that happened last night. I don't believe in destiny, but I feel there was a reason for us to meet. What do you think?"

"I think you're right."

"Can that night be the beginning of our friendship? I want to get to know you. You raise curiosity in my heart."

Even though Laurie had confessed to her mother and Anna that meeting with the bouncer was special in a certain way, she did not believe she'd made such a big impact on his heart just after two random kisses. She did not want to give him an emotional answer. Laurie quickly created a profile of the gentleman's personality. She already admired his calm. The gentleman did not seem to be aggressive and he behaved well. He showed a good level of respect and his request sounded simple.

Laurie replied, "That's a fair request and it is not a bad idea. We'll see."

The gentleman sighed and said, "Great." His persistence paid off.

Laurie did not intend to stay any longer and knew that he would have not minded to spend the rest of the evening with her.

"I was very happy to see you once again." She paused and continued, "To be honest with you, I didn't expect to see you tonight. Thanks a lot for your kindness."

"You're welcome. Thank you for spending some time with me tonight."

"By the way, if they say anything about last night, please let me know. The manager of *The Flow* is my friend."

"I will," the gentleman said before he took three steps towards her.

Laurie knew he wanted to wish her good night, but she was wondering how. She would have felt uncomfortable if he tried to kiss her. The gentleman had the ability to read people's eyes and understood her concern. So he opened his arms and hugged her instead — a choice that further revealed his personality.

"Wow! Your body is so warm," he called out.

"I know…and nobody wants to sleep with me because my body is too hot," Laurie replied with a bit of sadness on her voice.

The gentleman smiled and said to himself that she must be kidding. He could not stop himself from asking that question.

"Are you serious?"

"Yes I am, and it's bad," she replied.

"I wish I could just stay in your arms,"

The gentleman's last comment made her happy. She compressed her lips, glanced at him, and then she asked, "Do you want to hug me one more time before I leave?"

"You don't even have to ask. It will be always yes," the bouncer answered before he hastened to hold her in his arms.

Then he looked at her straight in the eyes and asked, "Will I get your number tonight?"

Laurie smiled at him and answered, "Don't worry about that."

He hugged her once again for over fifteen seconds. She held him tight. His cologne smelled so good she wanted to leave her head on his shoulder for the rest of the night.

There was something interesting between Laurie and the gentleman: whenever they got close to each other, they did not want to be separated. He could have insisted for her number, but he did not intend to put pressure on her freedom.

"Have a wonderful night. Kiss your mother and Anna for me please."

"Thanks. Have a great night and be careful."

The gentleman watched Laurie got into the elevator. He felt proud and satisfied after completing his mission. He put his hands into his pocket and proceeded to *The Flow* to start his work. When she reached her apartment, her mother and Anna were already in bed. Laurie took a shower and sat in the living room to watch a TV show.

Everything was perfect for the gentleman that night. Nobody said anything to him. More customers turned out in the bar that Saturday night; the hot weather mixed with a heavy air encouraged people to go out. The DJ played better, and both floors were opened. Customers, all sweaty, were drinking and dancing. They were having a good time.

As usual, Perez was chatting with some customers and smoking cigarettes with them. Anytime Perez saw a pretty lady, he held her ID, and told a joke to try to get her phone number. He was good at that. His charisma, eloquence, and warm welcome eased his way in catching women's attention.

The gentleman maintained his same professional attitude. He did not talk too much to the customers and kept everything simple. He spent most of his time patrolling the floors inside. Whenever some customers, especially the young ones, were acting crazy and doing nasty things, he flashed a light on them. If they were really acting out, he called Perez before making any moves. Those orders came from Carl who did not want the gentleman to be rough and harsh with some special customers who were considered the life of the party.

At 4:15 a.m., the bouncers closed the doors of *The Flow*. No incident occurred that night. They took a couple shots and left the bar. On their way, Perez told the gentleman he was lucky because the manager who reviewed the camera every morning did not see what happened. Perez advised his coworker to be more cautious next time. Perez drove his car home, and the gentleman took the trains back home.

During his trip home, the gentleman thought about his second meeting with Laurie. He came up with a pessimist answer about the likelihood for him and Laurie to start a relationship. He based it on three factors: first, she did not look at him often that Saturday night. Second, she gave him a diplomatic answer when he asked about starting a friendship with her. Even though she admitted that the gentleman deserved some credit, she still did not give him her phone number. And third, when she was entering the building, she never turned her head back. Once again, Perez' speech came back into his mind. But his heart convinced him that Laurie could be the one.

At 5:30 a.m., the gentleman reached his house composed of one living room, one small kitchen, one bathroom, and two bedrooms. His living room was painted in white with two paintings on the wall. It contained a bookshelf, a red couch, a 52-inch flat screen TV on the wall, a small table under the TV with a DVD player, a VCR, and some DVD's at the top. He crossed the living and went into his room where he undressed. Then he took a shower and went to bed.

JUNE 3, 2012

The gentleman woke up around 2:30 p.m. and ordered a ranchero burrito from a Mexican restaurant. Every Sunday, he liked to visit different places. He left his house around 4:45 p.m. with the Brooklyn Bridge as the destination in mind. While on the train he thought about the ambiance he saw yesterday in Washington Square Park. Once he arrived at Atlantic Avenue, he decided to go and explore the atmosphere of the park instead of the bridge.

The gentleman took the D train, got off at West 4th Street, and reached the park at 5:35 p.m. He found the park enjoyable. There were many people from different boroughs and tourists wandering in the park. Water was spraying from the fountain situated in the middle of the park, and parents were watching their kids having fun in the water. Some people were looking at their dogs playing while others were reading their books or playing chess.

It was relaxing on that hot afternoon with thick, humid air. The gentleman saw an arch built in memory of George Washington, and noticed that many people were on a date. The park projected such a beautiful picture that he fell in love with it right away.

Two different bands were entertaining the public with good music in each corner of the park. One band had a lead singer and the other one was strictly instrumental. Both bands performed like professionals and had their own crowd. Although the public showed love to the bands with tips, the performance of the bands was worth more than a couple of singles deposited in the baskets on the ground.

The dollars were not the motivation for the bands; their passion to entertain people enhanced their performance. There is no doubt New York City is one of the most expensive cities in the world. However, it makes anyone — rich, poor, or middle class — to dream. It can provide the same opportunities to success no matter what one's origin may be.

The gentleman was having a great time at Washington Square Park. After exploring the park, he stopped by the instrumental band. A few minutes later, someone tapped his back twice. When he turned his face, he saw Anna, Carlette, and Laurie. He shook his head and smiled because he was surprised to see them. He hugged and kissed them. They were happy to see him three days in a row. Anna, Carlette, and the gentleman exchanged words about their respective day. Laurie remained quiet for a couple of minutes, then came up with an idea, and said, "I think you should take some pictures together, guys."

"That's a nice idea. Take some with my phone. So I can post them on Facebook," Anna said.

"Then, let's take a walk in the park," Carlette added.

Laurie took a few pictures with Anna's phone by the arch. But she took none of her with the gentleman. Once they were done with the photo shoot, they strolled in pairs. Laurie was in front with Anna. Carlette was behind with the gentleman.

The gentleman was slick. Instead of walking next to Laurie, he walked with Carlette first. He wanted to know how Carlette felt about him. When dating a woman, her mother represents the easiest target and could become a great ally.

As Carlette started walking with the gentleman, she asked him, "Do you have a girlfriend?"

"No, I don't," the gentleman replied without hesitation.

Carlette glanced at him and said, "Laurie is also single. How come such a nice guy like you doesn't have a woman in his life?"

"I had a recent experience that didn't go well."

"Oh! I am sorry. You and Laurie are in the same boat." She paused and then asked, "Was it your fault?"

"I did my best. I was in love with her since the first day I saw her in December 1997. We were teens. I was happy my dream came true in May 2011, but our adventure didn't last long. She took another path."

"How did you feel after that?"

The gentleman sighed and confessed, "In the beginning, it was difficult. I had a hard time adjusting to the single life once again. You know, life is a school where you learn and experience different situations. It was good to try that relationship anyway."

"I like your positive way of thinking."

"Thanks."

"I hope you and Laurie will both find what you're looking for."

"I hope so."

Carlette provided a lot of advice to the gentleman about life, love, and relationships. She expressed herself with honesty in a calm voice. Meanwhile, Anna and Laurie were talking about life in New York City. Carlette and the gentleman had a mother-son conversation. Her speech was broad and she spoke like a master who wanted to transfer general knowledge to a chosen student.

After twenty-five minutes of walking, Carlette said,

"Anna! I want to sit for a little bit. You can continue with Laurie and him."

"Mom, let me keep you company," Laurie said. She wanted to make sure her mother was doing well.

"Ok, we'll come back soon," Anna said.

I Dare You To Try It

Carlette sat down on a bench and continued her advice with her daughter who listened carefully. Anna continued to stroll with the gentleman. In less than one minute, Anna asked, "What do you think about Laurie?"

That was the most interesting question. Anna was a direct person who liked to go straight to the point. She was much more direct than Carlette.

"I have met many women before, but none of them have captured my imagination way Laurie has. She's beautiful and possesses a magical smile. I would like to get to know her."

"Well said. Are you patient?"

"That's one of my faults."

"Do you think that you could start cultivating it?"

He took a deep breath and said, "I will try."

The gentleman had an impression something good was coming out of this. Like a road, the conversation started broad with Carlette and was getting narrower with Anna. Instead of telling, Anna questioned him. She wanted him to be aware of the importance for him to start a relationship with Laurie and fight to have Laurie's heart. After asking many questions, Anna gave some hints to the gentleman.

"Do you know that Carlette is a very difficult person? But for an unknown reason, she likes you."

"I am happy to know that."

"I don't know why, but I have a good feeling about you and Laurie."

"She's special. I think she injected something into my heart with her kisses," the gentleman said with a smile.

"I don't know your expectations and goals in life. I don't know how long you will be able to wait, but I pray that you can see what I see in Laurie, and for Laurie to see what I see in you."

Anna and the gentleman spent thirty minutes together before they joined Carlette and Laurie. Around 7:50 p.m., Anna, Carlette, Laurie, and the gentleman left the park. They headed toward Laurie's apartment. Anna and Carlette explained how much they enjoyed their vacation in New York City for its fun and entertainment.

"I would have never imagined my last days in New York would be this great," Carlette said

Anna looked at the gentleman and added, "I feel like we've known you for a long time."

Once they arrived in front of the building, they all stopped walking. Before they went upstairs, the gentleman kissed Anna and Carlette on their cheeks. He hugged them and said, "I had a wonderful time with you all since Friday. Have a nice trip and I hope to see you back soon in New York City."

"Thank you for your kindness," Carlette said.

"Remember what I told you," Anna added.

Both, Anna and Carlette took the elevators and went to apartment E13. Laurie looked boldly at the gentleman, and said,

"I guess this is our point of meeting. It's always you and me at the end."

"That's true," the gentleman replied with a smile.

"I saw my mother and Anna each gave you a speech. I think now it's my time to express myself in a few words."

"It would be a pleasure to listen to your words."

"Don't be too excited. I am not like them. It's just an observation."

"It's fine. Tell me. I would be happy to hear it."

"I discovered a fourth quality about you."

"Thanks. If you don't mind, can you please tell me what those four qualities are?"

"Sure."

Laurie looked the gentleman straight in his eyes before telling him the results of her observation.

"Number 1: You are calm, which means you can deal with stress. Number 2: You are a nice person. My mother and Anna like the way you treat them. Number 3: I have met many aggressive guys. I mean men who show me their sexual intention within minutes of approaching me. But you're not like them. Number 4: Last night, I did not turn back. I was looking through a mirror to see if you would have left just after I left, but you stayed and waited until I got into the elevator. That tells you are a true security guard — maybe someone I could rely on for protection."

The gentleman was surprised she was paying such close attention to him without demonstrating any sign of interest. Often, many people behave in any way they want without thinking that others are observing them. Every single person within an environment represents a camera that captures words and images.

"Wow, wow. I am speechless."

"Why? Am I wrong?" Laurie asked.

"No, you're not. You speak the truth. I would never imagine you were observing me to that point."

Man looks at and dreams about the physical appearance of a woman. Woman judges and decides based on the first words and actions of a man. First impressions can make evil look like an angel, and an angel look like forbidden fruit.

"Well. I am sorry, but you're not the only secret agent, Mr. Bond. After all, you look like a good person. We could be friends." She paused, glared at him, and asked with an ironic smile, but in a joking way, "Do you have a phone?"

"Of course, I do."

He dipped his left hand into his pocket and showed her the device. "Here, it is."

Laurie took his phone and registered her number. Then, she gave it back to him and said, "Now you know how to contact me."

He finally received the friendship's key and said, "Thanks."

She admired his patience, smiled at him, and said, "You're welcome."

"Call or text, which one do you prefer?" he asked.

"Mmm... Text will be better because I am a busy person. I could read and reply to your message whenever I am free."

"Sounds great."

"It's getting late so I have to go. It's already 8:15 p.m. It's mom's last night, and I want to spend time with her before she leaves. Tomorrow will be a long day for me at work. Definitely, I want to sleep early tonight."

"Thank you for making my weekend one I will remember forever. I'm more than happy to meet such a nice and beautiful woman like you. You amaze me. I wish you a wonderful night. And for sure I will text you."

"Thank you very much for your sweet words. Have a great night as well."

The gentleman still wanted to kiss Laurie once again, but realized that he would have to be patient. He hugged her for a minute and she leaned her head on his chest like he was her boyfriend. Definitely whenever they got closer to each other they felt something particular. He watched Laurie get on the elevator to go to her apartment, and then he walked to the train station, and went back home.

When Laurie reached her apartment, Anna and Carlette were packing their stuff for their trip back to Michigan. Laurie helped them arrange their things and Anna and Carlette seized the occasion to share with Laurie their thoughts about the gentleman. They made a summary of their conversation with him. Laurie listened to what they said, but she said little about him.

When Anna, Carlette, and Laurie were done packing, they showered, and went to their respective rooms. The gentleman reached his home at 9:30 p.m. He ate a bowl of cereal, took a shower, and went to bed.

What a weird coincidence, both Laurie and the gentleman went to bed around 9:50 p.m. Laurie lay on her belly and the gentleman on his back. They were listening to songs and thinking about that epic weekend and that unexpected meeting.

Laurie turned on her radio and listened to *"I could fall in love"* by Selena, then *"From this moment"* by Shania Twain, and followed by *"The first time ever I saw your face"* by Celine Dion. Sometimes when it comes to love, a woman lives in the past, enjoys the present, and does deep thinking about the future. Laurie reviewed the whole scenario in her mind.

Man, when his heart is touched, he sees the future. The gentleman was dreaming already about having Laurie as the protector and the doctor of his heart. He listened to an international radio station that played *"Entra in mi vida letra"* by Sin Bandera, then *" L'envie d'aimer"* by Les Dix Commandements, and followed by *"When I dream at night"* from Marc Anthony. At around 10:30 p.m., they both fell asleep.

JUNE 4, 2012

Early on Monday morning, Laurie drove her mother and Anna to LaGuardia Airport. Right before she arrived at her intended destination, she received a text message from the gentleman wishing Anna and Carlette a safe trip. He also asked Laurie to let him know when they would land in Michigan. Laurie passed the message to her mother and Anna. They appreciated the care he showed to them.

Laurie pulled over next to the main entrance gate of the airport, and then she opened the trunk, and grabbed the two bags. She handed one to her mother and the other one to Anna. Laurie confessed how much she enjoyed their short stay in New York and told them she wished they could have stayed longer with her. She hugged and kissed them before she left. Carlette managed to not shed tears and promised to visit her again on Thanksgiving. Laurie got into her car, waved goodbye, and smiled at them before she drove to *Pelito & Co.* on Wall Street.

Laurie sent a text to the gentleman during her lunch-break to tell him that Anna and Carlette reached their destination safely. Laurie and the gentleman both had great days at work. Before he went to sleep, he texted Laurie to wish her a good night.

From that moment on, the gentleman sent a text to Laurie twice a day: one text in the morning and one text in the evening. But she did not answer him.

They say the older a person gets the better that person understands life and the future; one becomes wise. Carlette never stopped asking her daughter about the bouncer. She had the impression he could be the man for her daughter. However, she could not make the choice for Laurie.

Carlette asked the same question every time she talked to her daughter, "What do you think about the gentleman?" Sometimes, she asked Laurie in different ways, "What do you think about your meeting with the bouncer at *The Flow*?" Or "The gentleman is very nice. Isn't he?" Or "I like the bouncer. He is an interesting man. How do you feel about him?"

Laurie always answered her mother that she found him okay, but she never elaborated on the meaning of that okay. After many days, she expressed herself, "Mom, I understand what you're saying, but I lost confidence in love. My heart needs time to heal."

Certain experiences leave deep scars in someone's heart. Those scars could impact forever one's lifestyle and mindset. As a mother and a woman, it saddened Carlette to see her only daughter not lucky in love. Carlette always showed love to her daughter. She sent flowers or chocolate to Laurie at least once a month. She managed well to fill that feeling of emptiness left by the misadventures of her daughter.

Fourteen days passed, and the gentleman was still hoping to receive a text message from Laurie's. Despite all, he did not consider himself involved in a one-way friendship. He gave her the benefit of the doubt based on the fact that she could have been busy at work or maybe she was not into texting.

JUNE 17, 2012

Laurie woke up around 10:00 a.m. with a sense of loneliness. She walked toward the living room and realized how quiet her apartment was. Her nice apartment comprised of two bedrooms, one living room, one large kitchen, one bathroom, and two closets to store items. She was a well-organized woman and kept her apartment clean.

Laurie glanced around to see where that feeling came from. She wandered in each room because she felt something or maybe someone was missing. It had already been six months since she was living alone, but it was the first time she experienced such discomfort. She turned the radio on to give life to her apartment, but it was useless.

Thirty minutes later, she showered, wrapped herself in a towel, and went into the kitchen for breakfast. She opened her refrigerator and stared blank at everything in it. All of a sudden, she lost her appetite and could not decide what to eat. Laurie took an apple, leaned against the fridge, and started eating. The muscles of her throat tightened. She could barely swallow. She felt sick, and nothing seemed to interest her. Emotionally, she had a break down. She was tired of the same routine every week: go to work Monday through Friday, clean her apartment on Saturday morning before wandering in Manhattan, and on Sunday, read books, call her mom, and prepare herself for work.

Laurie felt so alone at home that Sunday. She ate half of the apple before putting it on the kitchen table. Then she poured cereal and milk into a bowl and walked into the living room. She sat down on her purple sofa and turned on her flat screen, smart TV. She checked all the channels, but she found nothing interesting.

Laurie sighed and turned off the TV. With a sudden movement she stood up; her towel fell on the floor and she did not even spare a glance at it. She headed naked to her bedroom. She climbed into her queen size bed and covered herself with a big fluffy cream comforter.

For a moment, the thoughts of her past relationships raced through her mind. She fought to shove the unhappy thoughts away. Yet, her mind kept replaying the arguments she had with her last boyfriend, all the useless sacrifices she did to try to make it work, and the last time he touched her warm body. All these thoughts just made her feel worse. A few minutes later, a deep slumber came to her rescue.

Laurie slept for over two hours, but woke up with the same empty feeling. She wished to hear some comforting words. Unfortunately, her clean beige walls and her fancy chandelier could not pronounce a single word. As she was wondering what she could do to make herself happy, she realized that maybe a few minutes with a wonderful person could make her day and bring happiness back to her heart. She scanned in her head which friend she could call. Yet, none of them seemed fit to fill her particular needs.

Fifteen minutes later, she checked her Facebook page, but she found nothing interesting. Then she scrolled through the text messages on her phone and read carefully those sent by the bouncer. Laurie thought about the comfort she felt when wrapped in the bouncer's arms. The comfort of his muscles, the scent of lemon, bergamot, and grapefruit from his cologne, and the temptation in his eyes created a desire to see him.

She smirked, and she sent him a text to ask if he had a plan for the evening. She invited him to come and hangout with her for a little. It was her second text message since they exchanged their phone numbers.

The gentleman was working on a project on his laptop in his room when his phone indicated a new message. He hoped to hear from Laurie, but he did not expect she would have requested a meeting so soon. He accepted the invitation with excitement and texted her back to confirm he was coming. The gentleman arrived at her address at 6:45 p.m. and waited in front of the building.

Laurie took the elevator down to meet him. They greeted one another with a regular hug. Then she asked, "What do you want to do?"

The gentleman glanced at her with confusion. He thought she already had a plan. He sighed and proposed, "I think we should go to the park. You know, walk and talk a little bit. What do you think?"

She agreed to the idea and shrugged, "That's fine with me. Let's go."

Among many other options the gentleman had, he chose the park because he wanted to get to know Laurie a bit. Since it was their first date, the park gave a broad, less embarrassing, and more comfortable environment. Neither of them would have to look at each other's eyes.

They headed toward *Washington Square Park*. It was one of the good nights to be out. A soft and cool breeze was blowing in the eighty-two degree evening. The sky was beautiful with stars and a big moon. As usual, people were entertaining or being entertained. They strolled in the park and talked to each other.

After questioning Laurie about her week at work, the gentleman asked, "What's your favorite color?"

"Actually, I have two favorite colors: red and black. What about you?"

"I like sky blue."

"Do you like sports?" the gentleman continued.

"Yes I do. I like football, basketball, and baseball. And you?"

"I like football, basketball, soccer, car racing, and boxing."

That night was good. The conversation between Laurie and the gentleman was interesting. He maintained a stress-free dialogue with her by asking basic questions such as: how many countries she'd visited, what she liked to do for fun, what her favorite team was in each sport she likes, what kind of movies she likes, etc.

Each time he asked her a question; she answered him and asked him the same question. This approach helped Laurie manage the time and allowed her to know about the gentleman's preferences.

Their promenade lasted about an hour and a half. Then they spent a few more minutes together in front of the building where Laurie lived. They did their routine hug, but this one was different. She held him tighter this time, pressed her body against his chest, and had a sigh of relief. She glanced up at him, shrugged, smiled, and said with a sweet voice, "Thanks for coming."

At that moment, the gentleman had an impression she was dealing with some issues, but he did not dare to ask her any question. He grinned and said, "Pleasure was all mine."

Before she went into the building, she demanded the gentleman to text her when he reached home. They both were satisfied with their first date. Once he arrived at his home, he sent a text and wished her a wonderful night. But, she did not reply because she'd fallen asleep. From that evening on, she managed to text him as much as she could.

JUNE 24, 2012

The following week on a Sunday evening, Laurie and the bouncer went out for dinner at *Le Cordon Bleu* on 80 East 67th Street, a restaurant known for the quality of its wine and its neo classical architecture. He wore a black pair of shoes, a grey slim fit pants, and a red shirt. She wore a neutral color dress with oval eyelets and a thick brown fashionable belt with peep toe wedges. The gentleman waited five minutes before Laurie showed up.

Once they got into the restaurant, a waitress seated them at a table for two and took their order. Before serving the food, the waitress brought two glasses of wine to their table. They sipped their drinks and told each other stories about their personal lives including a few stories from their childhoods.

After ten minutes, the waitress brought a filet mignon for Laurie and a boneless strip steak for the gentleman. As they ate, they continued their dialogue. In the middle of their conversation, Laurie told him about another observation she'd made.

"Do you know that you have great writing skills?"

"Thanks," the gentleman answered with a wry smile.

"No. I am serious. You should be a poet. You amaze me by the way you write your text messages," she stated.

The gentleman put down his fork and knife on his plate, and sipped his wine. Then he gazed at her and said, "Not every man on earth is so blessed to be friends with an angel. I am happy that my texts make you smile."

Laurie rushed to grab her phone in her black purse. She raised her left hand as a stop sign, selected one of his text messages, and said, "Let me read you one. Listen to this."

She glanced at him, then looked at her phone, and read by mimicking his calm and sweet voice, "Your smile warms up my heart. When you hug me it seems like there is no sin on this planet. You give me thoughts of Eden. That day you kissed me I touched the sky. You're a divine creature." She paused, raised her chin, and added, "That's so sweet."

The gentleman smiled, didn't say a word, but winked flirtatiously at her, and continued to eat. Laurie gazed at him and said, "Not only do they make me smile, but I save them as well. Do you write like that to all the girls you've been with?"

"I love writing. It's my passion. I used to write them letters. Nowadays, it's all about texting and email. Technology takes over," before he shrugged.

She nodded. "That's so true. Now, we are so much into technology and people have become less romantic." She paused and then asked, "Did they write back to you when they received your letters?"

"Yes, they did. And I saved all those letters."

"That's nice," she said before she sighed and confessed in a sorrow voice, "Unfortunately, I don't have any letter from my ex-lovers."

He glared at her in stupefaction. Laurie gave him a wry smile before she raised her hands and clarified, "Of course, they wrote me sweet text messages through the phone. I mean... I mean... I never received a letter." She paused and continued, "I guess it's romantic to read words from the one you love right before you sleep. I wish I had a letter from one of my exes."

He answered her with a smile and sipped his wine once again. She decided to focus on her plate a little, but she was observing the gentleman and the people around them.

Laurie was a quiet lady who liked to listen more than she spoke. However, that Sunday she took the lead. She acted like a detective, asked questions, commented, and made observation. The gentleman was a little surprised by her attitude. She could not help herself from talking.

Five minutes later, she stated, "You are like a magnet. Something about you drives people to you especially women. I don't know why and what."

The gentleman never met a woman as clever as Laurie before. The results of her observation about him were always true. Some ladies said they liked his eyes, others liked his smile, and certain could not even describe what caused them to go to him. They recognized that he was a fun, nice, and handsome guy.

The gentleman did not know how to answer her. He wondered what could have pushed her make such a comment. He gazed at her and asked her in a curious tone, "Why did you say that?"

She answered in subdued tones, "That lady next to the painting keeps looking at you. The waitress is staring at you also. She keeps coming and asking us if everything is okay, but she's not doing that so often for the other customers. Even in the street, I saw many women looking at you." She paused, "I wonder if you could be faithful."

The gentleman looked at her, smiled, and replied, "You don't have to think about that."

Laurie did not go further into that subject. Instead, she finished her plate. As they were enjoying the desserts, he told her some funny jokes about a guy named Joe. The jokes made her laugh out loud. She advised him, "If you don't stop your jokes, they'll kick us out."

They spent about two hours at the restaurant before they went back to Thompson Street. On their way back, the gentleman told Laurie about a book he wrote and sent to a publishing company. He explained to her that he did not know why the publisher took so long to publish his manuscript.

She expressed her desire to read it. And then, he asked her to be his manager in a joking way, but deep inside he meant it. She found that idea interesting and gave him a positive answer. Since they both acknowledged that they always had good time together, so they agreed to go out the following weekend.

A taxi dropped them off in front of her building. They did their routine hug before Laurie headed to her apartment. Right before she made her second step into the building, he called out, "Laurie…"

She turned her head, and he confessed, "I love to spend time with you. Your beauty and your observation skills hold my mind captive. Your smile lights up my heart."

His confession froze her and touched the deepest part of her heart. Their faces were so close to each other. For an instant, a strong feeling travelled her entire body and produced a tingling sensation. She was tempted to kiss him, yet she controlled herself. She shook her head, sighed, and said, "You're a sweet man. You always make me blush with your words."

That night, the gentleman could have made his intention clearer, but he did not want to rush. He remembered that Anna advised him patience would be the key to open Laurie's heart. He stood straight in front of the doors with his hands dipped into his pockets, and watched her get into the elevator. Then, he headed to the train station and went back to his house.

When Laurie got into her apartment, she closed the door behind her and leaned against it. She compressed her lips, closed her eyes, and replayed in her mind the wonderful date she had with the bouncer. He was not one of the most handsome men on earth, but she found him intriguing and romantic.

After a couple of minutes, she walked into her room. Laurie took off her dress and then went to the bathroom to wash her make up off and brush her teeth. Once she was done, she went to her room and climbed up her bed. She put a pillow between her legs, held a bear in her arms, and fell asleep.

JUNE 29, 2012

For their third date, right before she left work, Laurie texted and proposed that they go to the movie. He found the idea more than interesting and looked forward to it. He did not want to miss any opportunity to be around her. He chose not to go to work that Friday night and called out sick at *Team Undercover*. The gentleman picked her up in front of her building around 8:40 p.m. Then they took a cab and went to 42nd Street.

They dressed casual. Laurie had a spaghetti strap summer dress above the knee with flip-flops. Her hair was highlighted with caramel streaks. She wore her hair down and curly. He wore slim fit blue jeans, a white V-neck t-shirt that exposed his body especially his well-built arms, and navy blue Nike sneakers.

They got to the movie theater around 9:00 p.m. They looked at the board and saw many movies that sounded interesting. He loved action movies, and she had preferred romance and drama movies. Both were thinking about which movie could be best suited for the night.

"Which one do you wanna watch?" he asked.

She shrugged. "I don't know... You can choose any one you like. I'll be fine with it."

"Ladies first, your choice will be mine."

"You're so sweet."

She took her eyes off of him and looked at the titles. "I would go for *Break Out*. I like a movie with dancing. What do you think?"

"Sounds great, that settles it. Let me go get the tickets then."

This movie would have been the last the gentleman would have chosen. Since he was being romantic and gallant, he accepted her choice and bought two tickets for the movie that would start at 9:25 p.m. Meanwhile, she told him that drinks and anything else were her treat.

Whenever Laurie and the gentleman went out, she always wanted to pay despite his objection. She was Miss Independent. She believed a man would fall in love quicker with a woman who could not only take care of herself, but could also create in his mind the idea of building together. Laurie took his order, then headed toward the counter, and purchased two large popcorns, one large Sprite for her and one large regular Coke for him.

I Dare You To Try It

They went in theater #12. They found seats in the last row. Laurie felt something for the gentleman, though nothing above or below the line of friendship. For an unknown reason, she found a great pleasure at challenging his attitude. Even though she sometimes let him take the lead when they were out on a date, it was always a calculating move by Laurie. Put a man to work and you will see what he is capable of.

The movie had a lot of amazing stunts and choreography. Everyone in the room seemed to enjoy it. After fifty minutes, Laurie put her head on the gentleman's right shoulder. He held her left hand until the end of the movie at 11:23 p.m. On their way out, he glanced at her and said, "You made a great choice. I loved the movie. What about you?"

"Yes I did. Especially, the way it ended."

Neither of them would ever bet that movie would have been so interesting and intriguing. "You have fine taste," he added.

Laurie loved the fact that the gentleman always complimented and praised her. He always treated her like a queen — something every single woman likes.

Once they reached the streets, they gazed at each other and smiled. That look meant that they did not want the night to end that soon.

"What would you like to do now?" He asked with a smile.

"I don't know." She paused, "Mmm... Maybe we could take a walk in the park. What do you think?"

"That's a nice idea. Let's go!"

They took a taxi and went to *Washington Square Park*. On their way, the gentleman said, "Let me tell you another joke about Joe."

She raised her hands in exasperation, "Oh my gosh! You and your Joe again." Then she looked at him with a wry smile and said, "Go ahead." She was coming to know and appreciate his humor.

"Joe was a well-known alcoholic living in a small town. He drank at least twelve beers every single day. One day after listening to a pastor preach, Joe decided to get baptized and follow Jesus Christ for the rest of his life. Everyone in the town was happy that Joe made such a decision in his life. The day of the christening, the pastor dipped Joe three times into water. He told Joe that his old habits just died, and that he would not be called Joe anymore because of his new life in Christ. The pastor told Joe that in the name of Jesus, his name Joe would be changed into Peter. The church cheered because they thought Joe would stop drinking beer. The most interesting part for Joe was when the pastor told him that he could change anything he wants if he believes and asks it in the name of Jesus. Joe, on his way back to his house, went to a bar and asked for a bucket of water and a beer. The bartender was shocked because he knew that Joe just got baptized and swore to never drink alcohol for the rest of his life. But, the bartender gave Joe what he asked for anyway."

The gentleman stopped telling the joke to Laurie and looked at her to increase the suspense, and then he said, "Guess what?"

"What?" Laurie called out.

He continued and said, "Joe dipped the beer into the bucket of water three times and said you are no longer called beer anymore. In the name of Jesus, now you are lemonade."

Laurie could not catch her breath; she was laughing hysterically. Even the taxi driver laughed and acknowledged the joke was good.

After arriving to their destination, the taxi driver stopped the car and said, "Forgive me if I sound disrespectful. You guys are one of the cutest couples who got into this car. May God bless you and help you keep this relationship forever."

The gentleman thanked the taxi driver and paid him. Neither Laurie nor the gentleman made any comment about what the taxi driver said. But deep inside, they both thought about it.

The sky was cloudy. According to the weather channel, there was a possibility of a rain shower in the city in the early Saturday morning hours. Once they got out of the taxi, they started strolling in the park.

There were only nine people in the park: two couples, one homeless man, and a family of four who appeared to be tourists. It was a wonderful night with a soft and cool breeze.

"I like to walk in the park at night when there are stars in the sky and a full moon, but there's nothing in the sky right now," Laurie said.

"New York City is full of stars. Maybe they're all booked tonight. I don't know where the stars are, but I can confirm where the moon is."

"Where is the moon?" She asked with a big smile on her face. She expected either a funny or romantic answer.

"The moon is next to me now, and I am talking to her."

"You make me melt with your words. You are the sweetest man I've ever met."

"I am just a mirror. I reflect who you are."

"I like spending time with you. You make me feel special."

"You are so special to me. From now on, I will call you Trinity."

Laurie looked at him and smirked. She found that nickname lovable. They stopped strolling after thirty minutes, sat down on one of the fountain's stairs to cool off, and watched the water splashing in the air.

Two minutes later, it started raining, the other people rushed to take cover under the arch. The gentleman looked at her straight in the eyes. He requested something from her in silence, and she knew that he was asking her to not run away from the rain. However, she wondered what was in his mind. He kept gazing at her. So she asked, "What?"

"Let's stay in the rain a little while. The Bible says rain is a blessing from God."

"From poet to priest, very nice," she said sarcastically.

She paused, glanced at him, and confessed, "So far you've never disappointed me with your plans. We can sit and receive a blessing for a few minutes. I remember those days when I used to play in the rain when I was a teenager."

As it started pouring, the gentleman stood up, extended his arms to help her stand on her feet. Then they got off the fountain. She thought he wanted to take cover beneath the arc until he said, "Let's do some *Break Out* moves from the movie we watched tonight while in the rain."

"Are you crazy? People who see us will think that we're acting like teenagers."

"Too often, people take life too serious. They pay too much attention to what others may say or think about them. They hold themselves captive in stress instead of being free with happiness. Let me help you set yourself free Trinity. For me, there is nobody else here. It's just you and I," he insisted as he started dancing.

"Wow! Wow! You got some moves. You should be in the movie."

"I'm already in a movie," he said.

"Which one?" she asked with a curious tone.

He stopped dancing for a moment, stared at her, and stated, "I am in the movie of your life, Trinity."

Laurie became speechless. He caught her attention with two phrases: "set yourself free" and "movie of your life". She already felt like she was in a fairy tale since meeting him. Laurie did not know how long the bouncer would last in her life, but he carved his name in her mind and her heart with every word and moment spent with her.

"That's very sweet of you, and you are a good actor so far," she said with a lovely smile.

"Come on, show me some moves. Show me what you got Trinity," he insisted.

"I can't. I am sorry. I.., I.., I don't know how to break dance. I only danced ballet and can do a few steps in tango," she said as she leaned against the fountain.

She was willing to try, but the way he danced impressed her. She did not want to look foolish. He took her hands and said, "You never know until you try."

Finally, Laurie surrendered to the temptation. She started shaking her head as warm up and she began to dance. She amazed him with every single move. He stared at her before he said, "If only you could borrow my eyes to see how beautiful you are."

The gentleman paused and then continued to say, "I wish it would rain every time I am with you and I had the power to turn every single drop into a kiss. So I could wet your entire body with love." She shook her head, smiled at him, and kept dancing. His words were taking effect deep in her heart.

They danced and laughed like kids. The most interesting part was that they did not have any music playing. They were dancing love with the beat of their hearts. Laurie could not believe that as a twenty-eight year old woman and an Assistant Director of Marketing at an investment bank on Wall Street, she was dancing in the rain at 12:35 a.m. in a park just for fun. During that moment, she tasted the freedom he was offering her.

They became so wet that their clothes became nearly see-through. After a couple of minutes, he held her hands, pulled her against him, and danced in a slow motion tango, pressing their bodies against each other.

Laurie trembled on his smooth movements that were like waves caressing rocks, and he kissed her. She trembled more and more when he touched her lips and kissed her neck. She could not resist anymore and snapped, "I wanna go home now."

"Okay Trinity," the gentleman replied and kissed her one more time.

They headed towards Thompson Street. None of them said a word. She leaned into him. She was thinking about her desire and her personal rules. When they got in front of the building, she gave him her keys, and she asked him to take the elevator with her to the fifth floor.

The gentleman opened the doors in the lobby and moved toward the elevator with her, entering her building for the first time. Laurie reached her apartment and stopped in front of her door. She made up her mind. She turned around, leaned against the door, and said, "I had a wonderful time with you tonight. It was amazing."

"We were in heaven," the gentleman stated with his hands dipped into his pockets.

"So, this is where I live. I hope we will have more fun as our friendship grows. Thank you so much. You are such a sweet man. Be careful on your way home and please text me to let me know when you're home," she said before she hugged him.

The gentleman understood that Laurie did not intend to go any further that night. He realized something was missing. He wondered what he might have said or did to make her change her mind. Because that was the second time she was turned on, but he could not step into the Promised Land. The gentleman was so close; he could taste it and smell it. He wanted to say more. However, he was a respectful man. He did not want to rush and mess up what he had accomplished so far in the relationship.

The gentleman gave her the keys back. He could read in her eyes that she had a different feeling for him. He managed to hide his disappointment and said with a shaky tone, "Thank you Trinity. I had a great night," before he turned and walked toward the elevator.

With her lips compressed for a few seconds, Laurie gazed at him edging away. She sighed and then said with a sweet and calm voice, "I like the way you kiss. It's romantic."

He turned his head back, smiled at her, and said, "I still taste your lips on mine."

She did not have the strength to look straight in his eyes, so she put her head down and smiled. As he turned his head back toward the elevator, he heard her sigh. He automatically recognized that was the moment for him to make the big step. She was about to open her door when he turned back and asked, "Have you ever tried the Italian kiss?"

"What? What kind of kiss is that?"

"I dare you to try it," he challenged her.

That date was supposed to be over. However, he brought that subject up which allowed him additional time. The Italian Kiss idea carried so much curiosity that Laurie without hesitation shrugged and said, "Of course, I would love to know that one. I am not afraid… especially of you."

If only she knew where that kiss could lead. He walked close to her and said, "Close your eyes and do nothing else."

Laurie did not even realize that she was still in the hallway. She surrendered to his proposition. The gentleman started to kiss her lips with an indescribable tenderness. She trembled every five seconds like she was on low electric shock.

That kiss turned her on. His fingers were lightly touching her sensitive skin. His touch sent shivers down her spine. She breathed fast and wanted to scream.

His heavenly touch and her strong desire overcame all her rules. She grabbed him, kicked the door with her foot, and pulled him inside. She took off his V-neck t-shirt and surrendered herself to him.

The gentleman knew his secret and powerful weapon always worked. He did not go to her bedroom. Instead, he moved her to her sofa. While kissing her, he took his sneakers and her dress off. Then, his fingers travelled slowly on her entire body, from her neck to toes. He took off her bra and her eyes remained closed. She breathed shallowly and continued to tremble. He continued to kiss her neck, and then he went down to her breasts where he stopped.

The gentleman combined and coordinated simultaneously three actions: first, he kissed one mound of her breast, then rolled the other one with his thumb and index finger, and with the other hand he gently squeezed her labia.

After three minutes he went lower. He slid his right middle finger into her panty and caressed the top of her clitoris with it. He also kissed her belly at the same time and discovered she had a tattoo of three roses on her left side.

Two minutes later, he extended his arms, rolled the mounds of her breasts once again with his thumb and index finger, and bit her labia Then he took her black lace thong off with his hands, and licked her clitoris with his tongue while his fingers caressed her breasts.

After a few minutes, the gentleman penetrated her. He could have caressed her a little more. But he remembered his experience with a girl who changed her mind while he was just about to go in after caressing her for over twenty minutes. He took the experience as a lesson, and decided to move more quickly this time with Laurie.

He did a mixture of caressing and penetrating moves that kept increasing Laurie's sensation. It was a marvelous sensation for her. At that point, his left hand was doing the back and forth on her leg or squeezing the flesh of her ass. His right hand was playing around the mound of her breast. She breathed fast and kept whispering in his ears, "It's good baby. I like it honey."

For forty-five minutes, the gentleman was painting love in and on Laurie. The slow in and out mixed with sweet touches and kisses brought to light his artistic skills in sex. Laurie screamed when she ejaculated and held him tight because it was the first time she experienced a true orgasm. He brought her to orgasm twice before he raced to the final lane and popped champagne. Once he was done, he sat down on the floor, leaned his head on her legs, and continued to caress her.

The gentleman woke up the wild side in Laurie. In less than five minutes, a strange sensation went through her entire body. She started breathing heavily. She was hot and light headed. She could not resist the pressure of her desire.

Laurie grabbed his left hand and rushed with him to her bedroom. Laurie pushed the gentleman on the bed. She climbed the bed and went on top of him. Laurie kissed his neck with tenderness, then his chest, and then bit every single pack of his belly

She kept going down, reached his torch, grabbed his well-endowed penis, and turned it on with a good head. Laurie took over in that second half where she made an impressive demonstration of her skills.

Once his torch reached his complete extension, Laurie went on it and took a perpendicular position. She was riding him at more than a thousand miles per minute. Whenever she was about to have an orgasm she held both of his shoulders tight. The gentleman grabbed her ass when she did the perpendicular face to face. And he held her waist to increase the pressure when it was perpendicular back to face. When Laurie's legs were tired, she lay on the bed and he went over her.

He did different positions with her, but she felt a greater pleasure when he took her from behind. He slapped her ass with his hand as if he was playing tennis, and her ass was the ball. That moment became intense with an indescribable sensation. She yelled, "Fuck me baby. Fuck me."

When sex is going wild, women's speech changes — they do not use fancy words. They say exactly what they want the man to do. He pressed on the accelerator until he made full quadrant. She put a pillow on her face and was moaning loud. When he saw that, he slowed down, and Laurie yelled, "Don't stop! Don't stop!"

That was the most difficult part in the game for him. He had to maintain the same speed and make sure she reached the final lane before him. Sex requires altruism. She wished he could have stayed inside her forever. Her moaning resonated in the entire apartment.

Five minutes after they were done, Laurie confessed, "You touch me with your words. I feel guilty because you can read through my eyes. When I am with you I don't say much because it seems like you know everything about me. Most important of all is that in your arms I feel secure."

She paused, gazed at him, smiled, and stated, "Tonight is one of the best moments of my life. You amaze me with every single thing you do."

The gentleman stared at her, but did not say a word. He kissed her one more time. He lay on his back and Laurie put her head on his chest. The gentleman was caressing her hair when they both fell asleep on the bed.

Around 6:00 a.m. on Saturday, the gentleman woke up, got dressed, and left a note on the pillow for Laurie. He did not want to wake her up. He went back to his house because he had to go to security training in Brooklyn at 9:00 a.m.

JUNE 30, 2012

Early that Saturday morning, the gentleman was taking a shower when he felt a burning sensation on his back. He came out of the bathroom wearing orange boxers with horizontal navy blue stripes. He went into the living room where his brother was sitting down on the red sofa with his laptop on his lap, and asked him, "Gaby, can you check and see what's on my back? When I was showering my skin was burning."

Gaby gave him a worried look. The gentleman turned around and bent down. Gaby glanced at his brother's back and mocked, "Man, you have many nail traces on your back. It looks like you were fighting with a female version of wolverine."

The gentleman stood up, raised an eyebrow, and sighed. "All right," before he headed to his room.

Gabriel, also known as Gaby or Gabe, glared at his brother edging away and wanted to ask him about the scratches on his back. But he remained silent. In that family, everyone respected each other's privacy. They told stories and shared secrets only when they wanted to. One thing was sure; Gabriel knew his brother would tell him sooner or later.

Gabriel and the gentleman loved each other very much. They maintained a healthy relationship as brothers. The gentleman and Gabriel liked to get together often, and they enjoyed going to bars, smoking hookah, and talking. They loved the nightlife the city offered.

The gentleman advised Gabriel and Gabriel listened, and vice versa. The gentleman was a little more social than his brother. Even though each of them had their own philosophy on life, they still respected each other's decisions.

After the death of their parents in a car accident in September 2002, they faced many obstacles and had strength to overcome all of them. The gentleman always did his best to take care of his little brother and to make sure he finished college. The gentleman had to work two jobs to provide for the needs of his brother and his own.

Gabriel was a quiet person with a great heart and a good observer. He had a passion for film and photography. Gabriel respected and loved his brother very much. Most important, he understood the sacrifices his older brother made in order for him to achieve his goals.

The gentleman got dressed and went to the kitchen. He had a cup of black coffee and ate a bagel with peanut butter. While rushing to get to the training on time, he almost burned his tongue. The gentleman grabbed a banana and left. On his way out, he patted Gabriel's head, and said, "See you later," before he closed the door behind him.

Gabriel nodded, "Cool," and continued working on a video project on his laptop.

Around 9:30 a.m., Laurie woke up. With her eyes closed, she slipped her hands delicately on her bed to touch the gentleman. But, he was not there. She thought he was taking a shower or watching TV in the living room. Laurie called him three times. She received no answer, and the house was quiet. At first, Laurie found that odd.

Three minutes later, she sat up in the bed, covered her breasts with a pillow, and then glanced around the room. For a moment, she got scared, wondering if he robbed her. She glanced at her dresser and saw all her jewelry remained untouched. She sighed and regained her calm. In her second thought, she wondered if he was trying to surprise her since he was a romantic man who always caught her attention.

As she tried to grab another pillow, she saw a note on it. Her eyes turned red with anger after reading the sheet of paper. She did not appreciate at all that the bouncer already left. She wished she could have woken up in his arms and made him breakfast. Besides, he mentioned no training to her last night. Laurie threw away the paper with frustration.

She climbed off her bed, went to the bathroom, brushed her teeth, and took a shower. After cleaning herself up, Laurie went to the living room. She sat down on her couch where she found twelve pages of a story written by the gentleman on the small table in the living room. She folded her arms and glanced at the table twice and then she decided to read it.

The story was a recapitulation of their relationship — from their first encounter until last night. He finished it with a *"to be continued..."* Unfortunately, it was not enough to calm her down. In her fury, she threw the pages in the air. Her face became red. She did not move from the couch and hoped he would call or text her. It was hopeless. His action disappointed her and took her appetite away.

Meanwhile, the gentleman could no longer wait for that training to be over because he wanted to hear Laurie's voice. According to the rules of the training, everyone had to turn off their cellphone once inside; they offered that training once a year at a military facility.

Although the gentleman was focused on what he was learning, his heart was all about Laurie. He felt he was breathing another air — an air that gave the smell of paradise. He became the happiest man in the world that morning.

Two hours later, someone rang Laurie's bell. Laurie took a deep breath. She thought maybe it was the gentleman who came back from his training. She stood up and grabbed the papers on the floor before she walked toward her door entrance and buzzed the person in. Her heart was pounding. She wanted to see him so bad she opened her door and stared at the hallway toward the elevators.

As she heard the *bing* sound from the elevator, her eyes widened. Disappointed, she called out, "Hey Barbara."

"What's up girl?" Barbara asked.

"Nothing much, pretty girl," Laurie answered with a fake smile.

Barbara hugged and kissed Laurie. Then they both went to sit down on the couch beside each other. Barbara wore a white button down shirt tucked into a knee length beige skirt with brown stiletto sandals. She carried a white and brown leather handbag.

"What's new?" Laurie asked.

"All work and no play."

"As usual darling," Laurie mocked.

"What are you up to today?"

"Nothing special, I just woke up." Laurie shrugged.

Barbara glanced at her friend worriedly and said, "Since your mother left, you haven't called or texted me. Did I do or say something to upset you?"

Laurie looked at Barbara, then wrapped her arms around her friend's neck, and reassured her, "No sweetheart. Not at all, I've just been busy."

Barbara and Laurie had been friends for years. They were so close that a simple look between them was enough to tell if things were right or wrong. They were more like sisters than friends. No matter the circumstances, they kept their friendship alive.

"One thing is for sure: you don't have the same smile. Something is bothering you. Girl, you know you can't lie to me. I know you better than you know yourself," Barbara said.

Barbara moved closer to Laurie, put her right hand on Laurie's left lap, and said, "I'm leaving tomorrow for Indonesia for four weeks. My boss and I have to go to make an audit at a production site of *Razor and Co*. So, tell me what's bothering you while I am still here and can help."

Laurie glanced at her friend and tried to avoid Barbara's question, "You travel a lot, girl. You're like an ambassador."

"I wish." Barbara paused and nodded, "Honestly, I love to travel and my audit team often has to go away to complete jobs. I came here to spend time with my lovely friend."

"That's so sweet of you. You can make anyone feel better with your sweet words. I bet if you were a guy, you'd definitely be a player," Laurie joked.

Barbara made eye contact with Laurie and stated with a firm tone, "No sweetheart if I was a man, I would be with Laurie. She would be my princess. I would love her and make her happy like no man ever did," as she stood up to head to the kitchen.

Laurie laughed out loud, "I like that." She paused and then broke the news, "By the way, I met a guy when my mom was here. He seems cool. He's a nice guy. He makes me smile with the sweet texts he sends me."

Barbara looked at her in stupefaction, opened her arms, hugged and kissed her friend, and then said, "Oh my gosh! Seriously Laurie?" She continued, "Tell me more... the whole story," as she sat down again on the sofa and stared at Laurie.

Barbara and Laurie had a model friendship. They shared emotions and secrets. Barbara never had to worry about what she told Laurie because Laurie would never say a word to anyone. Laurie was the guardian of her friend's confessions.

For a moment, the surprise visit from Barbara took Laurie's fury away. The excitement shown by Barbara following the news pushed Laurie to tell her all the details. She glanced down at the floor as she was looking for the best way to summarize her encounter with the gentleman. She took a deep breath, "Okay, Let me be clearer. I met him at *The Flow*. He's a bouncer. My mother and Anna like him and he's interesting."

Some women proclaim love while deep down in their hearts, it's all about opportunities. Most women choose a man based on his present or future financial status. The word bouncer did not meet any criteria for Barbara who was materialistic. Barbara did not choose friends for who they were, but for what they possessed. The word bouncer hit Barbara like a wrecking ball. For a few seconds, she thought she did not hear Laurie well. She snapped, "What? Are you kidding me? You're with a bouncer."

Laurie replied with a well-balanced tone of voice, "We went out a couple of times. We had fun. No man made me happy like that before. He's calm, a good guy, and I feel good in his arms."

Barbara looked at Laurie in disgust, shook her head, and asked, "Did you sleep with him?"

Laurie glanced at her and nodded. "Yes, we had sex once. It was last night." She paused and stared blankly at the wall as she was reliving the moment. She bit her bottom lip and then said, "It was epic." Then she shook her head, looked at Barbara again, and said, "I can't even describe it to you. By simply thinking about him makes me horny."

Laurie held her shoulders with her hands and continued with her eyes gazing at the wall in front of her, "My heart is consumed by his touch and kisses."

Barbara stared at her friend in silence. At that point, she understood that Laurie was in love with the bouncer. Barbara Babino was born in Alpena, Michigan, to an Italian family. She was petite and curvy with blonde hair that passed her shoulders and twenty-eight years old. Moving forward was her philosophy. The financial aspect in choosing a man was paramount for her.

Barbara always stated to her friends that there was a city for everything. Venice for love, Paris for lights, Los Angeles for fame, and New York City was the Money City. For her, it did not matter if someone was happy or not in a relationship as long as that person possessed many assets. Barbara moved closer to Laurie and stated, "Sweetheart, I understand the way you feel. It has been already thirteen months since Ricardo left you, and it's the first time you had sex with a man."

Before Barbara even finished her speech, a sentiment of guilt seized Laurie, "I am sorry Barbara. I don't know what took over my mind to kiss him that Friday night, and then sleep with him last night. I acted like a whore."

That was a moment of confession — even Barbara had to empty her mind and liberate her conscience. "Don't say that. I was worse than you. You were able to wait for thirteen months, but me I broke the rules after one week. I was so mad. I couldn't believe James left me two weeks before our wedding."

Barbara rolled her eyes, took a deep breath, twirling her hair with her finger, and confessed, "It was a Thursday night, I went to *Heaven* nightclub. You know, the one on 14th Street. I was so upset, I hated my life, and I felt like dying. It was so painful what James did. I drank a lot that night. On my way out, I could barely make it up the stairs. I opened the door of the bar to leave; I tripped and someone caught me. At first, I thought it was an angel because nobody was behind me. I turned my face to see who that person was. The guy smiled and said, *"Don't worry, everything is okay."* He helped me walk out. We sat down outside on the stairs of a building next to *Heaven* for a few minutes and talked. I told him how depressed I was, that I hated my life and gave him the reasons. He explained the beauty of life and all the things that someone must go through in this world. I cried that night. He was wisdom itself. I didn't know how to thank him for those words and what to give him in return. I went home with him. He was a son of Adonis, born for sex and caress. That night was wonderful," Barbara explained with a smirk on her face.

Laurie glanced at Barbara, "Wow" and then, asked, "Where is he now?"

Barbara found it hard to swallow the fact she had slept with a man and knew nothing about. She cleared her throat and shrugged. "I pray every day to see him once again. I wish I'd given him my number. He was a man of class, well dressed, and smelled good."

Barbara continued, "I had seen him in the VIP section surrounded by many people earlier in the night. He drove me home in a limo with his own driver. I think he is made of money. Maybe he is my soul mate."

"Wait a minute! You slept with him not because of what he said to you, but because you thought he was rich. Am I right?" Laurie asked as she gave her friend a surprised look.

Barbara turned her face to Laurie and said with an emotionless voice, "100% percent correct sweetheart. I learned from your experiences with Gaspard Leboeuf and Ricardo Monte. You better stop dreaming about that bouncer and move forward. When you are with your co-workers, will you introduce your boyfriend as a bouncer? Come on Laurie. You're better than that."

At first sight, Laurie thought Barbara was sympathizing with her. After hearing all those confessions about the rich stranger her friend met at *Heaven,* Laurie took defense of her choice.

"I know, but it's different. It's not about what he does, but who he is. I love the man inside."

Barbara looked Laurie straight in the eyes and said, "Girl, listen, remember when I told you Gaspard was a jerk, he simply wanted to sleep with you to forget about his past relationship. He used you as a rebound. You told me no. I said Ricardo was a bastard; he stayed with you for your money, but you didn't listen."

Laurie did not know what else to say to Barbara. If she had listened to her best friend maybe she would not have had to go through such difficult moments in her life with Gaspard and Ricardo. Quite often, Barbara's predictions were true.

Barbara was skilled in speech, a well-articulated woman, and persuasive. She continued to say, "We, women, are so innocent. We fall in love after a kiss and we start making plans for the future after hearing a couple of lies. Men win easily because they know our weaknesses. They make us believe we are the only girls in the world. They pretend they don't want anything. Men are ready to marry us, but in reality they just want to have fun and sleep with women. Once they reach their destination, they change, and then disappear."

Laurie explained to Barbara what the bouncer did to her this morning. Barbara advised her to take corrective action because it was a warning sign. In addition, the bouncer recently had experienced bad things in his last relationship. Laurie took a deep breath, glanced at Barbara, and said, "You are right, but…"

Barbara snapped, "There is no but. It will be your third man. I tried to prevent you from the first two. However, you did not want to listen. I never led you on the wrong path. I advise you like you were me. You should stop slacking off Laurie. I could kill any man who tries to play with your heart."

"No sweetheart, don't go that far," Laurie said as she squeezed her friend's hands.

Barbara insisted, "I am serious Laurie. You have no idea how much you mean to me. I can't see you cry anymore because of a jerk. You don't deserve such treatment. Also, this guy was in a relationship. He is heartbroken like you. My experience with James taught me that a relationship between two recent broken hearts can't last for long. Honey, the relationship with the bouncer will not work. Trust me."

At that point, Laurie had no more reason to defend the bouncer. While Laurie was thinking about all that was said, Barbara's alarm from her phone rang. Barbara stood up, took her purse, hugged, and kissed her, "Gotta go sweetheart. I have a meeting with my boss. Take good care of yourself. I will see you in four weeks."

As Barbara was edging away, Laurie called out, "Be careful over there. Have a safe trip. Thanks for stopping by before your trip. I'll miss you."

Barbara turned her head and responded, "I love you and I will miss you too. Remember, don't join the LLT."

Laurie glanced at her and asked, "What's LLT Barbara?"

Barbara replied with a wry smile, "Losers in Love Team."

Laurie smiled and said, "Only you, Barbara."

They laughed out loud. Laurie remained seated on the sofa. Barbara left the apartment and shut the door behind her on her way out. After deeply thinking about Barbara's comments, Laurie wrote the following three long text messages to the gentleman.

```
    I    have    received    your    sweet
messages, and I have read your beautiful
written   story   about   our   encounters.
Thank you for all. I am still uncertain
what  took  over  my  mind  and  heart  to
approach  you  that  night.  I  may  never
know, but I do know that I am grateful
that you are such a sweet man.
    Also I know that you were hurt by
love this past year and you still wear
that    tag    around    your    neck    that
```

represents that love. I also was hurt by love more recently and am still recovering. And as sweet as your heart and your words are, my heart is not ready to be involved again this soon. Over the past few days, I have tried to move past that pain, but being honest with myself I am not ready. I don't want to hurt you because of my own healing process I am going through.

I hope you can understand and we can stay in touch over the phone and perhaps take a walk in the park at a future date. Again, thank you for being such a sweet, sweet man. You have been an angel. Have a wonderful day. Please don't try to convince me. You are free to look for another girl who will love you and please you more than I do.

What a nice way to wish a man a wonderful day. At 4:00 p.m., the training was over. The gentleman was the first to rush in the lobby to retrieve his personal items. He told the security agent his name. The security guard handed the gentleman his belongings. He was happy to turn on his phone and became happier when he saw he received text messages from Laurie. He rushed to read them.

The seconds that followed his reading were almost his last time breathing. His mouth was open, but no air could get through his lungs. He stared blinking at the phone in his right hand. The gentleman read the messages once again. He was in denial and could not believe Laurie wrote him such messages after their great night together when she'd told him how he made her feel secure in love.

The gentleman lost his mind. Those text messages knocked him out. His knees became so weak that he did not have the strength to walk out of the building. He sighed and leaned against a wall.

The security agent looked at him worriedly and asked, "Sir, are you okay?" The gentleman nodded and took another deep breath before heading to his car.

As the gentleman was edging away, the guard kept his eyes on him. By the way he was walking out; the security agent could not stop himself from offering his help again to the young man in distress, "Are you sure you don't need any help, sir?"

The gentleman raised his right hand and made a sign with his thumb to tell him he was fine before he opened the door and let it slam behind him.

The security agent shook his head and understood that the gentleman received bad news. Since other trainees were coming to him for their items, he focused back to his job and continued the distribution.

When the gentleman got into his car, he reclined the driver seat, and put his arms behind his head. All of a sudden, his body temperature rose. He started sweating and then he became cold like ice. After forty minutes, he started his engine and drove back home.

Once he arrived home, he grabbed a bottle of water and went straight to his room. The gentleman climbed into his bed in desolation without even taking off his pair of sneakers. He lay on his belly and started meditating.

None of the girls he was with before, ever said he was not a good man. They all wished to have kids with him. Yet, one thing was hard for him to understand: the fact the girls always left him. He wondered why the women he loved and wanted to sacrifice everything to keep them were those who stayed the least. But those he did not love much were ready to die to have him.

The gentleman was like one of those greatest basketball players without ring. His comments and advice about women were at least ninety-five percent correct like he held the secret of women's playbook, no matter her background, her nationality, or her color.

Many young boys and even married men came to his house and listened to his advice whenever they faced a difficult situation involving a woman. They called him: *The man.* They saw him as a true player — the type who could tame any woman. The truth of his wisdom came from his obsession of three books in The Bible: the book of Proverbs, the book of Ecclesiastes, and the book of Song of Songs.

He believed Laurie was the one he should have met. The gentleman questioned himself about the reasons she wrote such text messages. He could not find any answer to this misfortune. The love between Laurie and the gentleman was going too fast, maybe. He fell from the sky and came back to his reality. In for a penny, in for a pound, he had to accept his fate.

That Saturday night was one of the longest nights for him. He could not sleep at all that night. There was a paramount question that the gentleman spent the whole time thinking about — why does a woman often leave a man after she had a great moment with him?

On Monday morning, the gentleman showed up at his primary job: *Maimonides Medical Center*. The hospital was located on 10th avenue and was considered the best cardiology hospital in New York.

He was always pleasant at work and tackling all assignments with dedication. However that Monday, all his co-workers saw that he was not himself. They approached him and asked what was going on, but he pretended everything was fine. Everyone saw he struggled to put a smile on his face.

At work, at the gym, and with his friends, his body was there, but his mind vanished in the universe. He wished to text her back many times. Yet, each of those times he could not find the correct words to express his disappointment or thoughts about such regards. He did not call her because he did not want to be too emotional and show his weakness. As a writer, he did what he knew would be the best thing to do. On Wednesday morning, the gentleman mailed a letter to Laurie.

Even after sending the letter, his mind was still racing with thoughts and his body was in agony. In less than four days, he lost over fifteen pounds. It was best diet plan ever. Water was the only thing he had a taste for. He took sleeping pills to kill his insomnia, but instead those pills kept him awake all night. He wished he was working on a night shift.

The gentleman needed a therapist or someone to help carry that burden, or even help him forget about Laurie for a few days. A simple phone call could have resolved his problem. Yet at that moment, none of the women who wanted to give him everything could fill the gap left by Laurie. The gentleman realized only time would heal his heart.

JULY 6, 2012

TGIF, 5:00 p.m., work was over. Laurie clocked out and ran to her car. She wanted to be home and lay down following a busy week at work. When she reached her car she realized seven days had passed, and she had not heard from the bouncer. She found that odd. She checked her phone, but there was no message. She could not believe it. She said to herself maybe her phone was not working properly.

Laurie turned the phone off then on. Suddenly, she heard a sound like a Facebook text message and she rushed to go on Facebook to read it. Unfortunately, it was just a friend saying hi. Laurie turned red; she wanted to throw her phone away.

Why did she feel like that when she asked the gentleman to slow down and be a simple friend? As Rene

Descartes, the French writer, said "the heart has it reasons that reason itself ignores." His text messages were like drugs to her soul; she needed them, and she had become addicted without realizing it.

The gentleman had his own unique way of touching her heart without making any incision. She was recovering, and as a patient, his words were like IV fluids that penetrated slowly and deeply in her heart. The tears falling down Laurie's cheeks were the only things that could describe her feeling.

Laurie called the bouncer, but she got his voicemail. She sent several texts, but received no answer. What a misfortune, because that Friday morning on his way to *Maimonides Medical Center*, the gentleman lost his phone. Laurie wanted to talk to a friend, but Barbara was not in New York City. She called Barbara anyway and left her a voice mail.

Laurie drove back and reached home around 6:45 p.m. She picked up her mail in the lobby, and took the elevator to the fifth floor to her apartment. Laurie was so upset that she did not pay attention to the mail. She opened her door, threw the mail on the floor in the living room. Laurie walked into her room, lay on her bed, and started to cry, "Oh my God! Why me? Am I cursed in love? I did everything I could to find true love."

Laurie cried more and more. Her bed became a pool of tears and her heart was in agony. In her mind, the bouncer betrayed her. Meanwhile, she made an emotional decision by texting the gentleman and asking him to become a simple friend. She expected he would have fought for her, texted or called to try to change her mind and build that love. Tired of crying, she fell asleep.

Three hours later, Laurie woke up with a new idea. She took a shower, got dressed, and went to *The Flow*. She thought when she got there; maybe she would see the gentleman. She became more than determined to see him that Friday night. She saw two bouncers; unfortunately neither of them were the gentleman. At that point, she lost hope. She decided to stay a little at the bar to kill her sorrow.

The gentleman was working at *Universal*, a nightclub on 13th Street in Manhattan. Around midnight, Marc-Allan Yurikov, the manager of *Team Undercover*, called the gentleman and asked him to go to *The Flow* because one of the bouncers from *The Flow* had gone to the hospital.

That night, DJ Ray was killing it. He was a well-known dj with a big student crowd. He also hosted a radio show every day from 4:00 p.m. to 6:00 p.m. Many people always turned out wherever he was playing. Carl had to make some runs to help Perez handle the crowd. Both floors of *The Flow* were full with people.

The gentleman left *Universal,* took a cab, and went to *The Flow*. It was the first time the gentleman came back to *The Flow* since the weekend he met Laurie. One thing was for sure, he was happy to work with Perez once again.

"Finally you're here man," Perez said as he shook the gentleman's right hand.

"Yeah man, I'm back."

"Yo man, tonight is crazy. We had to call an ambulance for Rony, the other security guard. Now, we have more people coming in. I hope they don't get drunk. Otherwise, it will be a tough night," Perez said.

"All right man. We will do our best. Everything will be fine. What happened to Rony?"

"I can't tell exactly... I was on the second floor when a customer ran and called out the bouncer had passed out. I ran outside and I found Rony on the ground surrounded by people. I was scared to death man. When the paramedic came they said his blood pressure and his heart rate dropped. They took him to the hospital."

The gentleman sighed, shook his head, and nodded. "Damn man."

Carl walked out as the gentleman was about to go in. Carl greeted him and said, "Hey buddy, nice to see you again." He paused and glanced at the bouncers, "It's a tough night guys. Perez you will go inside and you stay at the doors. All right guys, do your best. Thanks a lot. Now I am going to take care of some special customers." Carl gave the gentleman one walky-talky and then patted the shoulders of both bouncers before he went back inside.

Both bouncers agreed to Carl's decision. They shook hands and did what the manager asked them.

"Be careful man. If anything, call me," the gentleman said.

"Don't worry man. This is my house. I know most of the people who are inside. Take care bro," Perez replied before he went inside.

The gentleman did not have a chance to go inside. Around 1:30 a.m., Carl came outside and asked him, "Is everything okay buddy?"

"So far, all is good boss."

"Both floors are packed. How many people did you count so far?"

"238," the gentleman answered.

Carl glanced at the streets and then glanced at the gentleman, "You know what, don't let anyone else in when we reach 250, the maximum occupancy. I am not paying any ticket for that. If someone mentions my name, call me. I'll come out to see if I can let them get in or not. We have some faithful customers who spend a lot of money every Friday. They usually come around 2:00 a.m."

The gentleman nodded and remained focused on his duties. Carl went back inside.

Forty-five minutes later, two men were walking towards *The Flow*. They came from *The Click*, a strip club three blocks away. The gentleman had his back against the door and was checking a customer's ID when a man inside *The Flow* opened the door for a lady who appeared to be with him. The lady stepped out, the two men were walking in front of *The Flow* when all of a sudden, a man in a black Cadillac fired at the two men.

There was total chaos — everybody on the block ran. The customer whose ID was being check by the gentleman, laid flat on the ground. The guy who opened the door for the lady had two choices: close the door and stay inside or run to protect the lady. Charity begins at home. He chose the option of safety.

Quite often, when facing danger, the first reaction of a woman is to scream. One of the two men ran and fired back at the Cadillac. With an instinctive move, the gentleman jumped on the lady and wrapped her in his arms. He covered her like he was her bodyguard and went down with her behind a car. That was a crazy act by the gentleman. He put his life in danger for someone he did not know in a night worth only $100.

One of the two men fell on the ground and remained immobile. The other one ran toward *Washington Square Park*, and the Cadillac evaporated in the street.

"Oh my God! It's you. You save my life," said Laurie, the lady.

"It's okay. Everything will be fine," the bouncer said as he closed his eyes and unwrapped himself around her.

"Please call an ambulance. Call 911. He's shot. Somebody please call 911," Laurie screamed when she saw blood coming out from the bouncer's suit.

The gentleman was breathing shallowly and coughing up blood. His body became cold, and he trembled before he lost consciousness. Laurie, with eyes and mouth wide opened, shook when she saw blood coming out of his mouth. She thought he was about to die. The guy who'd opened the door for Laurie, made the call.

Perez ran out when someone said the security guard outside just got shot. His first picture of the scene was a woman sitting on the ground, crying, and holding the gentleman in her arms, broken glass from car windows next to them, and a man lying flat on the ground a couple of feet away. Fortunately for the customers on the first floor, the doors of *The Flow* were strong enough to contain the bullets. Everybody stayed inside *The Flow, and* DJ Ray stopped the music.

"Oh shit! Fuck! What happened?" Perez yelled as he took off his vest and covered the gentleman.

The two people who could explain the story to Perez were: the man who was providing information to 911 on the phone and Laurie who was crying.

Laurie held the head of the gentleman and said to him in a panicked voice, "Please say something. Open your eyes. Talk to me. Please don't die. Please, I need you. Please, talk to me."

It was a sad moment outside *The Flow*. Many people thought the gentleman was Laurie's husband or boyfriend. One thing is sure; no sacrifice is greater than one giving his life to save someone else.

An FDNY ambulance followed by three NYPD cars came in less than five minutes. The paramedics scanned the scene of the shooting — a young lady hysterically crying and holding a man in her arms, and a couple of feet away, a man lying in a pool of blood. A bullet hit his head and his brain was all over the place. He was pronounced dead right away by the medics. He was one of the two men targeted by the Cadillac.

As the EMT 4302 Team was providing first aid to the wounded bouncer, two NYPD cops outlined the crime scene with yellow tape. The cops blocked off the street from traffic with their cars and then questioned every single witness. Since Laurie could not stop crying, the guy who called 911 also provided insights to the cops about the shooting.

The gentleman was breathing with a faint pulse and bleeding profusely. The paramedic removed his clothes and controlled his bleeding. The bouncer was shot in the lungs and the shoulders. They checked his lungs and then used an occlusive dressing to release the pressure in the lungs.

After they stabilized him, they made sure there were no other wounds, and then they applied a cervical collar to him. They also gave him oxygen and placed him on a long board to prevent spinal injury. After putting him in the back of the ambulance, they inserted an intravenous line in his right arm to give him plenty of fluid, and put a breathing tube in his nose. The first responders did everything they had to do before they rushed to the closest trauma center.

Once the ambulance left, all that was left was the gentleman's blood seeping down the drainage system and his new pair of Kenneth Cole shoes lying on the ground reminding people of his sense of style. The cops continued to collect information about the incident.

Carl was shocked. He believed a major incident was meant to happen that night. After calling an ambulance for Rony, now it was the gentleman's turn to use an ambulance. He held his head with his hands as he was answering a couple of questions from the cops.

Laurie gazed at her bloody hands, and her body was shaking. She became inconsolable. Perez walked toward her, then held her in his arms, and tried to comfort her in silence by patting her back. While standing next to Laurie, he realized he was lucky and his internal voice kept saying, *"It could have been me, it could have been me."*

As soon as Laurie regained some of her composure, she said to Perez, "I wanna go home."

He glanced at her and asked, "Do you want me to walk you to your home?" She raised her chin and nodded. Perez held her left arm and escorted her to her building. He dropped her in front of the elevators and then he went back to *The Flow*.

Laurie reached her living room in desolation with her dress painted in blood and fell on the sofa. She could not believe what just happened. She was devastated by the regret of not confessing to the gentleman that she loved him and wanted him back in her life. Laurie was in tears and feared the worst — he might die on his way to the hospital after losing so much blood.

The incident kept coming to her mind, haunting her; she knew her night would be complicated. Finally, Laurie stood up, went in her kitchen, and grabbed a bottle of vodka. She went back to the living room, took off her shoes, sat down on the floor, and started drinking. She winced each time she put the bottle in her mouth. The vodka was too strong for her stomach and she never drank it straight like that before. Since she was drinking fast, the alcohol quickly drained into her blood, and a major headache hit her.

Laurie grabbed her head with her hands and started pulling her hair like her head was about to explode. She wanted to scream, but no words would come out of her mouth. After a few minutes, Laurie threw up on the carpet where she sat and then fell asleep on the floor. That sleep was a big relief for Laurie.

When facing an obstacle in life, people may drink and smoke as much as they want to erase pain. Yet, the problem will remain unsolved because alcohol, drugs, or cigarettes will never fix anything.

Thirty minutes after they transported the gentleman to *Santa Philomena Hospital*, all the customers left *The Flow*. Carl called Marc-Allan to report what had happened in front of the bar. Around 3:30 a.m., every employee of *The Flow* went home.

After calling the hospital, Carl called Marc-Allan again to break the news about the condition of the bouncer. The bouncer received four bullets: two on his left lung, one that just missed his heart, and one in his left shoulder. He underwent surgery to remove the bullets. The gentleman was alive, but in critical condition. Fifteen minutes later, Marc-Allan called Gabriel to give him insight about the incident.

One hour later, Gabriel reached the hospital and spoke with Doctor Sergey Sadiq. After that conversation, Gabriel went back to his house. He put clothes in a gym bag, grabbed his laptop and some books and notebooks, and then he went back to the hospital.

JULY 7, 2012

The incident was already part of the Saturday morning breaking news. Mikelson Shamaib, a worldwide well-known journalist working for *NYC News* was visiting his family in White Plains on his last weekend of vacation. He was watching the news when he saw that the shooting happened in front of *The Flow*. His house was across the street and facing *The Flow*.

Mikelson took his car and drove back to West 3rd Street. Once he reached his house, he reviewed his three outside cameras. One camera faced toward the train station, another one facing the bar, and a third one provided images from Thompson Street. Mikelson watched the whole shooting, and then brought the tape to his workplace.

Laurie woke up around 1:15 p.m. on Saturday and still felt the migraine. Her apartment was quiet. For a few minutes, she stared at the mess she made in her living room and the empty bottle lying next to her. She wiped her mouth with the back of her left hand and walked like a zombie toward the kitchen.

Laurie acknowledged that a cold shower could have helped her. But, she could not afford such luxury because she could barely stand on her feet. She grabbed a chair, ate two slices of bread, then took one bottle of water from the fridge, and headed to her bedroom. She jumped on her bed and fell back to sleep until the following day.

At 7:30 p.m., the *NYC News* made a special report about the shooting. Many people called *NYC News*, tweeted, and posted on Facebook their thoughts about the bouncer. Some qualified the bouncer as the most foolish man in the world while others saw him as a hero. Many people on social media asked more information about the woman saved by the bouncer.

This incident became so interesting that *NYC News'* administrative staff kept the story going for the entire week. On Sunday night, they aired a special report about the shooting from 8:00 p.m. to 8:30 p.m. They named it: *A Hero Among Us*.

On Monday morning, Laurie called out sick and requested two weeks off of work. Her supervisor told her to take as much time as she needed to recover because there were two summer interns to fill her position. The supervisor also advised Laurie to consult a mental health care provider. Laurie could not keep up with the stress. It was a total confusion for her. The one who supposedly betrayed her in love was the one who saved her life.

On Wednesday night, they invited Marc-Allan to the 8:00pm show on *NYC News*. He talked about his company and stated that any of his employees would have done the same thing as the gentleman did to save the lady. The boss of *Team Undercover* who barely interacted with his employees, praised the qualities of the gentleman and affirmed he considered him as a brother.

Before the show ended, Marc-Allan received phone calls, texts messages, and emails from different restaurants, bars, and nightclubs that wanted to hire bouncers from *Team Undercover*. "One man's poison is another man's medicine."

JULY 13, 2012

Eight days following the shooting, on Friday afternoon, Gabriel was sitting backwards on a chair with his arms on the headrest in the room where his wounded brother was surrounded by machines. Gabriel stared at his brother with a million thoughts and unanswered questions in his mind. The most disturbing ones were the following: *Would my brother make it?* Eight days have passed and the gentleman was on the breathing machine and still could not pronounce a word. *How long will my brother have to use that ventilator?* Even though the doctors gave Gabriel some encouraging answers about his brother's status, he feared the worst when the thoughts of the scene from the movie *Million Dollar Baby* came into his mind. Maggie was doomed to use the breathing machine. *How my brother and I would be able to pay off the hospital bills?* Gabriel was not working. *Who would pay for the rent? How are we going to afford the prescriptions?*

Gabriel understood that it became a must for him to find a job. He thought maybe he could work at *Maimonides Medical Center* in his brother's position and maybe Marc-Allan would grant him the same favor. Even if he found a job in both companies he wondered who would stay with his brother.

A few minutes later, two men wearing black suits and white shirts walked in the room. One had a loose red tie and the other one without any. They came to pay a visit to the bouncer at the hospital. They were tall, big, and chunky. At first, Gabriel thought they were his brother's co-workers until the man without a tie extended his right hand to him and said, "Marc-Allan and this is my assistant Thiery."

"Gabriel."

"Oh! You're his brother. We spoke on the phone after the incident," Marc-Allan said before he dipped his hands into his pockets.

"Yup," Gabriel answered before he folded his arms and then nodded.

Marc-Allan glanced over at the entire room and then said, "Your brother is a lucky man. Do you know that?"

"I guess," Gabriel replied.

Marc-Allan glared at the bouncer in silence for two minutes, sighed, and then he took a book of checks out of the pocket of his suit. He wrote a check, handed it to

Gabriel, and said, "This is for your brother." Then, he turned toward the doors and was about to leave.

Gabriel glanced at the check, then stood up, and demanded, "That's it?" He became frustrated when he saw the check he received was for only $500.

Marc-Allan stopped walking, turned his head back, and retorted with a firm voice, "It was supposed to be $200 for Friday and Saturday at any cost. I gave him $500 for Friday only."

"I assume the media got you more deals. Now you're making more money with new contracts because of him. Aren't you?" He paused, "You said you considered him as a brother. Is this the way you treat your family members?" Gabriel demanded.

"Listen boy. Go to someone else to teach your conscience's lessons. Open your eyes. This is USA, the country of opportunities. I understand your concern, but I am a businessman. Take it or leave it," Marc-Allan said with arrogance.

Gabriel's first thought was to tear the check into pieces and then throw it in Marc-Allan's face. No matter the situation, one should always think and act wisely when facing obstacles or having anger burning inside because every action carries its consequences. In that situation, humility was Gabriel's best set-play. He shook his head, put the check in his pocket, and did not add any other words. But in his eyes, anyone could see a flame of anger and disappointment.

Despite all, Gabriel had to take the check because he knew his brother had no insurance. At least with that money, he could buy some prescriptions or maybe he could find another $400 to add to it and pay their rent that was due in six days.

Thiery remained quiet during the entire conversation between his boss and Gabriel. His face was unreadable. He stood straight with his arms crossed on his chest and his eyes were scanning the room. Marc-Allan gave him an eyebrow and he understood his boss's gesture meant that it was time for them to leave. On his way out, Thiery patted Gabriel's left shoulder and said, "Take care buddy," as he followed his boss and slammed the door behind him.

Gabriel was in his last semester at Eagle University located on Varrick Street. He was enrolled in a Bachelor degree program in photography and film. He had classes three days a week: Monday, Tuesday, and Thursday from 1:00 p.m. to 5:00 p.m. After his brother got shot, to go to school, Gabriel walked three miles to and from school. Fortunately for Gabriel, it was summer, but the sun was burning him a little. He tried to travel the least possible to save more money.

Besides going to school, Gabriel was always in the hospital room where his brother was admitted. One of the hospital's housekeepers gave him a blanket so he could sleep on a chair at night. Since his brother could not eat, Gabriel ate the hospital food.

On Saturday, Carlette came back to New York City to stay and support her daughter mentally and emotionally. Laurie was down in the dumps. Carlette sent flowers and a card to the gentleman at the hospital on Sunday. However, she did not have the strength to go see the one who jeopardized his life to save her daughter's life.

People kept asking about the lady the bouncer saved. They wanted to know what she felt at that moment. The media was doing its best to find out the identity of that woman and reveal it to the public. During an interview, Carl and Perez stated that the lady was a random customer, and they did not have any information about her.

JULY 16, 2012

On Monday morning, Gabriel went to *Maimonides Medical Center* where he met his brother's supervisor, Elizabeth Guerrero. She came from Cuba. She immigrated the United States when she was five years old. Elizabeth was a person with a great heart and very friendly.

Gabriel told her all the financial problems he was facing and explained everything to her. Elizabeth sympathized with him and said that she would talk to the manager in the Human Resources to see if they could hire him during his brother's absence. She was surprised that the gentleman did not enroll with the insurance company that came in April 2012 to the hospital.

Elizabeth told Gabriel if his brother had enrolled with the insurance company for only $45 every two weeks, the insurance would have paid his medical expenses up to $100,000. Also they would have given him a check every month for six months during his disability period. That information aggravated Gabriel. He wondered why his brother, who used to be so clever, did not enroll with the insurance company. Even though his expectations were not met immediately, Gabriel was positive they would hire him.

In the evening, *A Hero Among Us* tv Show took another dimension in its second week when an anonymous bouncer called and explained all risks that security guards faced with low wages and no insurance. Every revolution needs a martyr to start, and the gentleman was the one.

The following days, many security guards grouped themselves into committees to discuss about how they could create a union to protect security agents in New York City. In many other cities like Los Angeles and Miami, there was a peaceful walk by many citizens to advocate for a raise and better treatment for security guards.

Many politicians expressed their thoughts about the subject. These politicians used that incident to build their campaign and made promises of change about the matter. That TV show turned many people into a social movement led by marginalized group.

Three days later, Elizabeth called Gabriel and told him they could not hire him because the gentleman was a biller, and Gabriel did not have any knowledge in that field. He decided against his will to contact Marc-Allan for work. The manager of *Team Undercover* required a valid New

York State security guard license. Both jobs were available Gabriel. However, he did not meet any of these criteria.

Gabriel used to pray every night before he slept. However that night, he shed tears on his blanket during his prayer. Besides those two failures, it was also his birthday. He wondered why life was so rough to his family. He was ten years old; the last time he blew candles out on a cake. He endured so many difficulties.

The doctors looked worried when they came to deal with the gentleman who kept having complications. They knew that they provided good treatment to the bouncer, but they also think they would be lucky if he was not disabled. Gabriel was scared to lose his brother.

JULY 19, 2012

Thursday afternoon around 2:40 p.m., the director of *NYC News,* Clair Zayas, received a call from the director of *PEN and INK Edition* about a book. At 8:00 p.m., the next day, there was something new to the show: the bouncer wrote a novel entitled *"Guilty of Natural Beauty."*

The book that the gentleman had been told Laurie about was not a joke after all. He finished the novel over a year ago. He could not find any agent to represent him, so he sent it to a publisher that accepted unsolicited submissions. *PEN and INK Edition* received the manuscript on November 2011. They published it two days before the shooting, but they did not do a big advertisement for it.

Mikelson and Evelina Mastroianni who hosted the show, talked about how interesting the book was. They stated they thought they were reading a movie script because the story was so detailed and dramatic. Evelina even confessed that she shed tears at the end of the novel. The book did not only carry a good story, but also its title intrigued people and made them buy it. The new subject to the show was: *How a woman could be guilty because of her beauty?*

The next two days, *Guilty of Natural Beauty* ran out of stock. *PEN and INK Edition* that did not want to advertise the book the months before because the author was unknown, was now making more money than ever. Everybody wanted to know about the bouncer and read his book. He raised curiosity in people's mind — a writer who became bouncer — a bouncer who became a hero.

Two weeks later, after many complications, the bouncer was finally able to sit. They took him off the ventilator, and he began his respiratory therapy. He had sores on his back. That Sunday afternoon, July 21, 2012 was a memorable day for all surgeons at *Santa Philomena Hospital*.

A few days later, he started walking, but was still having difficulty to breath. The gentleman appreciated all the sweet and comforting words he received from friends, co-workers, and hospital staff. A nurse came twice a day to clean the bouncer and applied new dressing on his wounds

Within ten days, seven million books were already sold online and in bookstores. The gentleman became famous. From now on, every single day the media called

Santa Philomena Hospital to know when the bouncer would be out. So they could cover the event and interview him. The room where the gentleman was admitted became a botanical garden. So many people, people who did not even know him, sent him cards and flowers. But his heart was ached because he hoped to read a few words from Laurie. He never stopped talking to Gabriel about her.

Gabriel wondered if his brother was not still in shock after that incident. He thought the gentleman would need a mental treatment as well. Gabriel felt that he would need to find the wolverine lady for his brother who was going nuts about her. Gabriel kept encouraging his wounded brother to remain patient and told him that Laurie would visit him soon.

JULY 31, 2012

On Tuesday morning, Carlette was doing a deep cleaning in Laurie's apartment when she found a letter on the floor of the living room among many others under the TV stand. She gave it to Laurie who was lying down on the couch. Her daughter glanced at it and gave it back to her. Carlette insisted that her daughter read the letter like she knew something about it. When Carlette realized Laurie did not intend to read the letter, she put it on Laurie's chest. She looked Laurie in the eyes and said, "If I were you I would read the letter," before she focused once again on the cleaning.

Laurie refused to open that letter because it was from the gentleman. She had enough of that relationship with the bouncer. She thought in her mind she almost caused his death. If she had listened once again to Barbara she would not experience such carnage. His blood in her hands and the brain of the other man spilled all over the sidewalk was haunting her. She was depressed. She took sleeping pills every day. Mentally, sleep was the best and her only way out.

Laurie stared at the envelope for over two minutes and then she put it in the shredder without even opening it. Fortunately, the shredder was full; it could not take any more paper. Therefore, she left it on the shredder. She went back on the couch where she laid down and then fell asleep a couple of minutes later.

When Laurie woke up, she turned on the TV. It was the first time she did that since that Friday night when she almost died. She was watching the news. She became aware of *Guilty of Natural Beauty*. Also Laurie found out that the gentleman would come out from the coma room for the first time since he was admitted to *Santa Philomena Hospital*. And there were different media outlets that wanted to cover the event.

She stood up and walked toward the shredder to get the mail. But the mail was already gone. There was no paper in the shredder. She said to herself this relationship was not meant to be. She heard her mother frying something in the kitchen. By curiosity, she headed to the kitchen and asked, "Mom, where is the mail that was above the shredder?"

I Dare You To Try It

"Which mail you're talking about?" Carlette said.

"The one you gave me," Laurie said as leaned on the refrigerator.

"I emptied the shredder and I put the bag in the trash area," Carlette answered.

Laurie compressed her lips, remained silent, and then she went back in the living room. Her mind was disturbed because her intuition kept telling her to go look for the letter. Finally, she ran downstairs to search for the mail among all those garbage bags that were deposited in the recycle area.

The super of the building was shocked to see Laurie opening all bags that contained papers. "Excuse me miss, have you lost something?" he asked politely. She nodded and continued to go crazy over all the dirty bags. He stared at her for a few seconds, shrugged, and disappeared.

When Laurie found the letter, she opened it with excitement. For a moment, she forgot she was in the recycle area; she sat down on one of the garbage bags, and read the letter:

```
Dear Laurie,

I did not want to text you. I chose
to   express   my   feeling   with   my
handwriting. I understand what you
wrote. I am sorry, but I can't let you
go so quick.
```

Please stay and don't go far away. I need you. I am pretty sure that I can make you smile and I am in love with your smile. Give me a try. I want to know you more. I can help you recover faster.

How could I not love you when you left the taste of your lips on mine and the traces of your caress on my entire body? You make me feel like I've never felt before. You brought love back to my heart.

Like you, I don't know why you kissed me that Friday night. I am not a man of faith and I don't believe in destiny. So many unbelievers in NYC and I am one of them, but I feel something different for you.

Have you ever thought about the first weekend we met? Why me? Why I could find you so easily? Why everything is so smooth between your mother, Anna, and I?

I know you may not have the answers. Let me stay close to you, be my cure as an angel, and light up my heart since you are Beautiful.

Laurie, I don't want to be with anyone else. I want to be with you. I want you to be my love. When the cold of life will try to take my happiness away and make me feel earth is hell, I want to be next to you so your hot body will comfort me. Your smile holds my heart and soul captive. I am happy because you are my Sunshine.

I love you Trinity.

Laurie ran back to her apartment. She ordered her mother to get dressed and go with her to *Santa Philomena Hospital*. She became so happy like she just got her freedom. Carlette could not understand that sudden change from her daughter. So she asked, "What happened Laurie? Are you okay sweetheart? What did you find out about him?"

Laurie did not answer her mother. She gave her the letter. After reading it, Carlette smiled and held Laurie tight. With a shock of excitement, she kissed her daughter. They took a shower and went to the hospital.

That same day Barbara came back to New York City from Indonesia because she was sick. She could not eat anything without throwing up. The smell of food was enough to make her feel sick. She could have gone to any hospital in Indonesia. But she believed only the doctors in the U.S were qualified and also possessed the equipment to treat patients.

Once she got off the plane, she went to her apartment to drop off her luggage, and then took a cab to the emergency room of *Santa Philomena Hospital*. They had her go through a series of exams. After ten minutes of waiting, a doctor came to Barbara and said, "Excuse me Miss Barbara. My name is Doctor Wladimir. All tests came back okay. We saw nothing wrong. Maybe you caught a food virus. Before I prescribe you any medication, I want you to take a pregnancy test."

Barbara was shocked with such a request from the doctor. She nodded, "Okay doctor."

The man that Barbara met at *Heaven* was the only man she had slept with since her fiancé left. All of a sudden, there was breaking news on the television and Barbara could not believe her eyes; the man she slept with was on the TV. It was noisy in the emergency room and she was far from the TV. She simply saw images of the scene. The only thing she could hear was that he was shot and to her surprise he was a bouncer. In the middle of confusion, she panicked and started talking to herself.

"Oh my God! What have I done? I slept with a bouncer! And now, I'm pregnant by his broke ass," Barbara called out with a frustrated voice.

"Are you okay? Whom are you talking to?" Doctor Wladimir asked politely.

"That bouncer who got shot. I think I'm having his kid," Barbara replied with an anxious voice.

"Really... Stay calm miss. You didn't even take the pregnancy test yet. Let's get the result first and take it from there," Doctor Wladimir advised her before he went to examine another patient. Barbara buried her head in her hands and asked herself what she would do if she was pregnant by a bouncer.

There was a woman sitting next to Barbara's bed. She was in the emergency room as well with her uncle who had a heart attack earlier. She overheard the conversation between Barbara and Doctor Wladimir. She could not help herself from breaking the news to the disappointed stranger. The woman glanced at Barbara and said with a calm voice, "I'm sorry and... I know I should have minded my business, but I think... you should consider yourself lucky if you are... pregnant by him."

"Why?" Barbara snapped.

"Hmmm... He's a writer. They sold more than 10 million copies of his book within one week while he was still in a coma. He's famous now and today he's going to talk for the first time to the media. That's why you see so many journalists at the hospital today. I even bought the book myself," the woman said as she showed the book to Barbara.

Barbara took the book, glanced at its title, and saw the picture of the man she met in *Heaven nightclub* on the back of the book. She said, "Are you serious? He's in this hospital?" The woman nodded and Barbara added, "You must be kidding. How do you know all that?"

"Do you live in a bubble? This story has been all over the news for weeks," the woman snapped before she said, "A good friend of mine who works in this hospital. She told me that within the next ten minutes the bouncer should be speaking on the 4th floor from the Intensive Care Unit."

Barbara called Laurie and left her a voice mail to come to the hospital as soon as possible because she needed someone by her side. She ran up to the 4th floor. She did not even thank the woman.

This week was stressful for every single employee of *Santa Philomena Hospital*. There was no margin for mistakes or negligence. The management staff of *Santa Philomena Hospital* granted authorization to reporters to visit some rooms and departments in the hospital. It was unbelievable to see how many patients and other people in the waiting area reading *"Guilty of Natural Beauty."*

The reporters interviewed patients, visitors, doctors, nurses, and other staff about the bouncer. Most of them said he was a hero and they hoped to have the pleasure of meeting him. He was like a motivation for them.

Carlette and Laurie were in the waiting area when a woman in white lab coat ran in the lobby and said, "Doctor Moskovits, we need you right now in room 415."

"Who is in room 415?" Doctor Moskovits asked.

"The healer."

I Dare You To Try It

Doctor Frankel Moskovits was one of the best pulmonary surgeons in New York. He had just returned from a trip to Cancun and had not met the gentleman yet. He took the elevator and ran into room 415 to check on the healer. The healer was a code name used by *Santa Philomena Hospital*'s staff for the bouncer to eliminate attention about his physical status.

Carlette could read in the employee's face and understood that something was wrong. She listened to her intuition and said, "Laurie, go ask this doctor about who the healer is. I feel like she is talking about the gentleman."

"Mom, don't worry. Stay calm. It's normal. We're in a hospital so they have to use codes."

"I know sweetheart... But how could the healer be in a room? It doesn't make any sense. Why do all the employees at the hospital look panicked? There is no doubt it must be him. Let's go and talk to the doctor," Carlette insisted.

Laurie did not want to resist her mother's intuition. Against her will, she walked over to the woman in the white lab coat and asked, "Excuse me doctor, can you please tell me who the healer is?"

"I'm not a doctor. I'm a physician assistant. My name is Fabiola. It's just a code we use at the hospital for certain emergencies."

Carlette was not satisfied with that answer from Fabiola. She said, "Okay great. Listen, my name is Carlette. Here is my daughter Laurie, the woman the bouncer saved.

Please tell us the truth. This is the first time she has stepped out since the incident."

Suddenly, all cameras turned on Laurie. They never saw her before and nobody knew if she was in the hospital because she wore a gray hoody and covered her head. There was a cemetery silence after Carlette said Laurie's name in the reception area. Everybody was waiting for Fabiola to break the news.

Fabiola was surprised to see Laurie and did not know what to say to her. As a woman, she could feel the pain of Laurie and as a physician assistant Fabiola should stay professional. Even though Fabiola did not know the two women, she had a feeling they were good people. She did not want to lie. So she said to Laurie, "Just go in room 415."

"Go Laurie. Go and see what's going on" Carlette insisted.

Laurie ran upstairs. Fabiola shook her head and hid her face between her hands. Thus, everyone present at that moment knew something was happening with the bouncer. All journalists followed Laurie up the stairs.

Both, Barbara and Laurie, were going to the gentleman's room. Barbara took the elevator and Laurie took the stairs. Barbara reached the room a couple of seconds before Laurie did. Laurie turned the corner to walk into the room and saw Barbara jump on the gentleman, kiss him, and say, "My love, I think of you each morning and dream of you every night."

Laurie was shocked and confused. She could not say a word and could not understand what was happening. She knew that Barbara was materialistic. So there was no way that Barbara could be friends with a bouncer.

A few seconds later, Barbara realized Laurie was in the room. Barbara thought her best friend came because she heard the voicemail. She said, "Laurie, thank God you're here." She paused and asked, "How did you get here so fast? I just left you the message."

Laurie looked at her confused and answered, "I never got your message."

"If you never got my message, what are you doing here?" Barbara asked.

Laurie stared at her friend in silence and wondered the reason of Barbara's presence in the room.

"Why don't you listen to my voicemail and find out? Go ahead. Play it on speaker, so he could listen to it also," Barbara said.

Laurie looked at her friend in disgust and played the voicemail on speaker. Everyone was listening to the voicemail and heard Barbara rambling and said:

"Laurie, oh my God, you're never gonna believe this. I got sick in Indonesia and I came back today. While I'm sitting in the hospital, I saw the man I told you about on the TV. He's the bouncer that got shot. The one everyone is talking about! And... oh my God, Laurie

I'm pregnant. I'm gonna have his baby. Now, I am in the emergency room of Santa Philomena Hospital. I'm about to see him in room 415 to break the news. I love him so much and I couldn't wait to see him."

"That's so sweet," said Jessica Cato, one of the nurses.

Although the gentleman remembered Barbara's face, he could not believe that she was pregnant. Besides Carlette, nobody else knew about the relationship between Laurie and the bouncer. So the voicemail did not seem strange to anyone else. To everybody else, Laurie was the random woman the gentleman saved and Barbara was his pregnant girlfriend.

Laurie stared at the gentleman and Barbara, but no words could come out her mouth. Barbara took her phone from her bag and said, "Oh Laurie, I have a voice mail from you also. Let me play it."

"Barbara, I've been thinking and as usual you're right. The bouncer is no good for me. He's not worth my time. I can't stand him. I wish I could erase the moments I spent with this fucking poor bouncer. When you get this message, call me."

Before anyone could say anything, the gentleman looked at Laurie, and spoke for the first time. He repeated what he just heard from Laurie's voice mail to Barbara,

"I am a fucking poor bouncer? Hmmm…"

At that moment, everybody was shocked. They understood what was going on between Barbara, Laurie, and the bouncer. Laurie stared at Barbara and the gentleman in silence as tears filled her eyes.

"What! Are you kidding me now?" Jessica exclaimed.

Laurie felt that Barbara betrayed her. Barbara advised her to not be with the bouncer and now Barbara claimed to be pregnant by him. Laurie became speechless. She looked at Barbara straight in her eyes with her mouth open. Laurie thought she was having a nightmare. She ran out of the room to the lobby to go join her mother. She was only thinking of the way Barbara stabbed her in the back.

"I was such a fool to not give you my phone number. I'm sorry baby," Barbara said to the gentleman as she caressed his face.

"It's okay whatever happened, happened for a reason," the gentleman snapped.

He was upset to hear what Laurie said about him. Quite often people neglect the power of words. Laurie forgot to use hers with wisdom. One sentence is enough to turn love into hate, cause more damage in a person than any other threat, and even destroy one's life forever. The gentleman felt a twinge of conscience for his heroic act.

Doctors asked everyone to leave the room because the gentleman's blood pressure and heart rate were elevated. He started breathing heavily. Barbara kissed him and said, "I'm not going far. If you need me, I'll be right outside the door."

Everyone left the room and doctors tried to stabilize the bouncer. Some journalists followed Laurie and others stayed with Barbara. The reporters broadcasted the event live like a reality TV show.

Carlette watched the entire scene that occurred between Barbara, Laurie, and the gentleman. She could not take the suspense anymore. Her blood pressure rose and she fell on the floor in the reception room.

When Laurie went down in the lobby, she could not find her mother. While she was looking for her mother, Fabiola came and told Laurie that Carlette fainted, and they took her to the emergency room. Laurie was scared when she received the news about her mother. She went straight to the emergency room and saw Carlette lying on a bed.

Barbara saw a young man in his early twenties standing behind the door next to her. She said, "I'm Barbara."

"Gabriel, his brother."

"Nice to meet you. Since the first night I set eyes on your brother, I fell in love with him."

Gabriel nodded and said nothing about that statement. Barbara started to describe the gentleman and say so many good things about him. But deep inside, she knew she was guessing and lying about the bouncer's personality. She spent a few hours with him and she was tipsy. That night the gentleman first met Barbara; he left a great impression on her. But she did not know the truth about him.

Heaven was a nightclub made for a certain group of people — the rich people. At the door, it was $50 for women and $100 for men to come in. The cheapest drinks started at $50. At *Heaven*, they did not sell beer. Bottles of liquors started at $2,000. If someone was inside that club that meant that person had some financial capabilities. *Heaven* required a dress code from its customers. Barbara had seen the class in the gentleman's attitude. In addition to smelling good, the gentleman was stylish. His 6 foot 2 inches frame made him look like a model.

The gentleman used to work at *Heaven* as a bouncer. Thus, he had access to it. Bartenders at *Heaven* knew him well, so they gave him free drinks. The limousine that picked him and Barbara up to bring them to Barbara's apartment was driven by his cousin, Samuel. Samuel's boss was also at *Heaven* that night. The gentleman simply had to text his cousin and to ask him for a ride. Samuel gave a lot of respect to the gentleman. He acted like the gentleman was his boss. Advising people was something innate in the gentleman.

The green envy that dwelled in Barbara's mind blocked her wisdom and decreased her capability to make good judgment about people. Barbara wanted to engage

Gabriel more in the conversation. So she asked him, "Do you want coffee?"

"No thanks," Gabriel replied.

Barbara also talked about her job and her trip to Indonesia. Gabriel did not want to be rude; therefore, he pretended to pay her attention. He was more worried about his brother's health than her stories. After ten minutes, Barbara realized that Gabriel was not interested about her stories and remained silent.

Journalists kept asking Laurie questions about her relationship with Barbara and the bouncer. Security guards of *Santa Philomena Hospital* had to escort these journalists out from the emergency room because it was causing too much chaos. After being kicked out of the emergency room, the journalists went to the 4th floor to harass Barbara with questions. The situation took another dimension. The security agents had to escort all journalists outside the facility. It was too much to handle.

Fabiola and Doctor Wladimir took charge of Carlette and provided her with the care needed. There was an office on the 2nd floor that was used by fellows and residents; Fabiola put Laurie in that room so she could be away from people then went back to the emergency room. Laurie was inconsolable. After fifteen minutes, Fabiola came back to Laurie and said, "Doctor Wladimir said your mother is doing well. She forgot to take her medication this morning. She needs to rest and tomorrow morning she could go home."

"Thanks a lot," Laurie replied.

"You're welcome. She's in room 302 now. I will personally take care of her. You don't have to worry," Fabiola continued.

"I really appreciate what you are doing for us."

"Something deep inside of me is telling me you would have done the same for me."

"It seems like you're the only one person who doesn't judge me after what just happened in room 415," Laurie said with a guilty face

"There is no reason to judge. We, women, are very emotional. Sometimes we say or do things without thinking."

"You're right."

"If you don't mind me asking, do you love him?"

"He is like a drug and very addictive. He makes you feel good when you are with him and low without him. He makes me feel like no one ever made me feel before. I was upset with something he did and I left that stupid voicemail for her."

Often when asking people about the reasons they love someone, their answer is: because I love him or love her. People play smart — they do not want to be trapped in their own answers. Sometime lies sound way better than the truth. Honestly, between humans there is no free love. People affirm reasons they are with someone by stating qualities they are looking for in others. People, who know what qualities they are looking for, make better decisions, and find quicker solutions when it comes to fighting or leaving a relationship.

"I think you should try to talk to him and tell him what you feel," Fabiola advised.

"I guess it's too late," Laurie said.

"C'mon. Keep your chin up. Better late than never,"

"Get real. Everyone knows that the other girl is pregnant with his baby. And they watched the scene that happened upstairs. I don't want to complicate my life," Laurie replied.

"Oh boy," Fabiola added.

Fabiola and Laurie added no other word to their dialogue. Fabiola sipped her coffee. Laurie put her head against a table that was in the room. After five minutes of silence, Fabiola said, "Here is my cell phone number, call me if you need anything. Try to sleep because you really need to."

"Ok thanks again. I am fine," Laurie replied.

Fabiola went back to the emergency room to take care of other patients. Every fifteen minutes she checked on Carlette. She was also responsible for the gentleman. Fabiola was a caring person. She gained admiration from her peers because she was great at her job. But most of all, she was doing what she was born to do. Fabiola saw Barbara many times that night, but she never had a conversation with her for an unknown reason.

Barbara listened to the voicemail sent by Laurie when she was on her way to the emergency room. She

I Dare You To Try It

pretended to see it for the first time and replay it because she understood the connection between Laurie and the gentleman. She thought Laurie's voicemail would break them apart. The plan worked out well for Barbara. She had to choose between giving up on the gentleman and save her friendship with Laurie or marry him and live a rich life.

That same night Barbara became aware of the entire shooting scene. She knew that the gentleman saved Laurie and he was the bouncer whom Laurie talked about. Barbara saw nothing wrong with her action. After all, she met him before Laurie did and reached room 415 first. The early bird catches the worm.

The next day, early in the morning, Carlette and Laurie left the hospital and went back home. Barbara made up her mind and decided to make plays. First, she changed her phone number. Second, she disconnected her Facebook account. She also thought about moving to another apartment. All those actions by Barbara had one goal: keep Laurie as far away as possible. Best friends can become worst enemies over money, power, a man or a woman.

Later that afternoon, Barbara came back to *Santa Philomena Hospital* to visit the bouncer. When she reached the room, she hugged Gabriel and kissed the gentleman. Barbara asked Gabriel about his brother's physical condition. Gabriel told her in few words what doctors said to him about his brother's health.

After ten minutes, the gentleman asked, "So Laurie is your friend?"

"Yes and I would say she was my best friend," Barbara answered.

"Why would you say she was?" the gentleman asked.

"Because I told her about you and she said she was dating a man, but she never told me it was you. Now I realize what kind of friend she was."

"Why didn't you call her and ask her about all this?" the gentleman asked.

"There's no point to do that. She lied to me and she called you a poor bouncer. It's over between me and her."

The gentleman remained quiet when Barbara mentioned the words — poor bouncer. At that moment, Barbara discovered a secret, she would simply have to play with the bouncer's pride to keep him away and make him forget about Laurie. Barbara explained many other things that happened between Laurie and her during their friendship. And she told him she had enough.

Security at *Santa Philomena Hospital* was at the highest level since the whole incident in room 415. They added some police officers to maintain order and keep patients privacy.

The 8:00 p.m. show on *NY News* became more interesting. The new subject to the show was: *After sex, what's next?* From now on, Laurie's personality was taking a big hit. People were pissed off by the fact that Laurie slept with the boyfriend of her best friend and showed that much ingratitude to that same man who saved her life.

On Friday afternoon, August 3, *World Class*

Entertainment, one of the best producers of TV shows in New York contacted Barbara, Laurie and the gentleman about their desire to make this situation a reality TV show. Barbara agreed to the idea. Laurie rejected the project. For Laurie her privacy was paramount. The gentleman found the idea of reality TV show not interesting. He stated that he was a writer not an actor, but if both Barbara and Laurie agreed, he could try.

The following days, Barbara showered the gentleman with gifts. Every day after work, she came and spent time with him at the hospital. All those moves by Barbara blinded the gentleman's eyes and hid all her tricks. He could not see that Barbara was green with envy.

The bouncer was all over the news for an additional week and photos of Barbara and Laurie were on the front pages of newspapers that week. More people were buying the book written by the bouncer. From bouncer to hero, then hero to bestseller who slept with two best friends.

AUGUST 6, 2012

On Monday morning, Laurie had to go back to work. Around 8:50 a.m., she reached her workplace. Everyone was happy to see her back at work. They showered her with care and affection. But no one dared to ask Laurie questions about her relationship with Barbara and the bouncer, saying only "Welcome back or we miss you." Laurie appreciated the warm welcome she received. She went to her desk, turned on her computer, opened Microsoft Outlook, and read her e-mails. Meanwhile, the board members were holding a meeting in the conference room with Vicki Gikas Afua, the director of marketing of *Pelito & Co.* They discussed the impact that Laurie could possibly have on the revenues of the company.

Media was hounding the employees of *Pelito & Co* when they found out Laurie's identity. It was difficult for clients to go in and out the building. Laurie's presence was causing too much of a commotion. The board stated that many companies called and said they would no longer do business with *Pelito & Co* if Laurie remained as assistant director of marketing. Therefore, the board had to decide.

Vicki was a lovely woman born in New Jersey from a Greek mother and a Haitian father. She had a heart of gold and was always happy. She knew how to talk to every single person. Employees did not like it at all when she was absent or on vacation. She was an advisor; she treated people well, and talked like a mother to everyone at *Pelito & Co*. Vicki was the only female employee at the bank who never stressed out about anything. No matter what the case was, she always managed it. Most of all, everyone loved her because she always stepped up to protect an employee.

At the meeting, Vicki became aware that the board had decided to fire Laurie. As usual, she tried to make the board members change their minds. She glanced at each board member and said, "In less than six months, Laurie showed so many talents. And I remember everyone was praising her professional attitude. Listen you can't do that to her. She is heartbroken after all she has been through for the past two weeks. How will she be able to take care of herself? It's not fair. Why don't we create another position for her or switch her with another employee? I thought we were a family here."

"I understand and we acknowledge Laurie's dedication. Remember this place works because we are a family, but we need customers to bring money in, so we can continue taking care of the family," said Junior Mannino, the president of the board.

"She's a great worker and a great asset. She secured so many contracts for the company and now we're going to just drop her like that?" Vicki pleaded.

"I'm sorry Miss Vicki, but remember we are the board and you, her supervisor. If you don't agree with our decision feel free to find a new job," Junior added.

Junior Mannino was one of the most respected people at *Pelito & Co.* Since he took over the board three years ago after his father stepped down, the company gained more revenues. Employees received better benefits and pay rates. Junior owned sixty-three percent of the company. He ruled the board. Nobody had done before what he did in terms of better benefits for the employees of *Pelito & Co.* He was a genius in investment and capital market. Whatever he said became the rule. He was strict and did not talk much. Junior instilled fear in everyone who dealt with him. Whoever wanted to stand against him was given the axe within a week.

Vicki kept her mouth shut because Junior was a dictator. She knew how difficult it was to find a job in this economy. Although she loved Laurie, she had a family of two girls and a boy to take care of. Also, she received a good paycheck with many benefits for her position.

Ten minutes later, Junior called Laurie and asked her to come into the conference room. Laurie had no idea what was waiting for her. She would have never thought it was her last day at work. Laurie left her desk and went into the conference room. It was a rectangular room with a big round table in the middle that could seat twenty-four people. There was a dry erase board attached to the wall, a computer in the left end inside, a projector attached to the ceiling, and a big flat screen on the grey wall.

Once Laurie walked in the room, she greeted everyone with a big smile, and said, "Good morning." They replied like a choir, "Good morning Laurie."

She was surprised to see all the board members waiting for her. There were eleven people including Vicki, sitting around the table. She wondered what kind of surprise they had for her. She was excited and felt something good was on its way.

"Have a seat Miss Laurie," Junior ordered.

"Thank you," she replied with delight.

"We are happy to see you and we hope you're coping well with your private life," Junior continued with a calm voice.

"Thanks a lot, I appreciate your concern, Mr. Mannino," Laurie added politely.

"Laurie, we really appreciate your enthusiasm and dedication for this company. However, based on the circumstances we won't be able to keep you as assistant director of marketing. We've started to lose some important clients," Junior stated.

"What does that mean?" Laurie asked with a confused look as she glanced at everyone present in the boardroom.

At first, she thought they were about to put her in a lower position because they were not able to afford her salary. Or maybe they were trying to find an arrangement with her to decrease her salary.

"We've decided to move forward without you," Junior answered with a cold voice.

Laurie was shocked after Junior's statement. Yet, she tried to show them her will to stay. She continued, "But... I wouldn't mind a pay cut as long as I secure my job."

Everyone stared at Laurie, but Vicki kept her head down and could not look at her assistant begging in vain. The silent treatment let Laurie understand there was no point in arguing and the decision was already made.

She said, "I remember Vicki guaranteeing that I could remain in that position because everybody has liked the way I work," as she glanced at her immediate supervisor whose head was still facing the table.

"Yes, she meant it. Yet the board decided differently. Since we don't have any other open positions now, we will keep in touch with you. Once something is available, we will contact you," Junior added.

Laurie's eyes were filled with tears, but she managed to not let any roll down her cheeks. She could not believe that they fired her. Her life was falling apart.

Laurie glanced at the board members for a last time; she sighed, and then nodded. She put her work ID on the table, left the conference room, and went back to her desk. She grabbed all her things in her cubicle and loaded them into her car. Laurie's co-workers were shocked when they became aware of what happened to her with the board. They wondered why they let her come to work when they could have emailed or called her to break the news. Life brings adversities that could make people give up on life, but one must remain strong. In front of some difficult times only the strongest will survive.

Vicki left the boardroom and went to Laurie's desk. She hugged Laurie and said, "Be strong my girl. I'm positive that God will open a door for you. Stay in touch with me. I will do my best and ask some friends in other companies."

"Thanks," Laurie said as she glanced at her powerless supervisor who continued to avoid eye contact with her.

Every co-worker hugged her and encouraged her to remain strong. Laurie drove back home as soon as she finished loading all her things in her car. As she was driving, she realized that her calvary had just begun. Immersed into deep thoughts, she did not stop at a red light. One cop followed her immediately. Laurie pulled over when she heard the cop car's siren.

"License and registration please," the cop asked.

The cop received what he asked of the driver. He saw a young beautiful lady with tears falling down her cheeks.

Her nose was wet from all the crying. At first, he thought she was acting like that to avoid getting a ticket. The cop took Laurie's driving documents and went to his car. He checked and did not find any bad report about her.

As he started writing the violation ticket, the image of the young beautiful lady in desolation came to his mind. He wondered what could be so painful to her. He went back to her, but could not keep himself from asking, "Are you okay miss?"

Laurie chose not to hide her deception. She glanced at the cop, shook her head, and answered, "They fired me."

Her tears touched his heart. He scratched his head, sighed, and said, "I'll let you go, but you gotta promise me you will pay attention to the lights. Otherwise you'll do more harm to yourself and other innocent people," as he handed Laurie her documents. The cop did not want to add more punishment to what was already inflicted to the young lady.

Laurie nodded and mumbled, "Thanks, I will… officer."

The cop walked back to his car. Laurie continued her itinerary and made sure to respect the traffic lights. She found a spot right across the building where she lived. She parked her car, took only her purse, and went to her apartment, with tears still rolling down her cheeks. Laurie went straight to her bed. She lay flat on her belly, buried her head in a pillow, and continued crying.

Carlette was washing the dishes when Laurie came

back. She found her daughter's quick return odd. Therefore, she went to Laurie's bedroom to check on her. She stopped right at the door and said, "You're already back sweetheart. How was it?"

Since she did not receive an answer, Carlette went to sit on the bed and realized that Laurie was crying. She rubbed her daughter's back and asked, "What happened honey? Why are you crying?"

"I'm sorry mom, but it's so painful. Now, I lost my job. What am I going to do?"

"Don't worry darling. God knows everything and he is able," Carlette comforted her.

Laurie turned on her side, put her head on her mother's lap, and said, "Barbara advised me to leave him and now she is pregnant by him." Laurie was more affected by the loss of the bouncer than her job. She could always find another job, but she was not sure when and if she would ever meet a man like the gentleman again.

"I really liked him. He seemed like such a nice guy. I thought you guys would have made a great couple," Carlette stated.

"Yes I thought so too, but he would cheat all the time. All those times, Barbara and him were together, but I couldn't see that. Now, I understand the reason she told me to let him go. She wanted to be with him. What a bitch."

"Don't judge too quick, honey. Wait and see if she will call you."

In a short amount of time, the bouncer had gained so

much love and respect from Carlette. She could not pronounce any negative word about him even though her daughter was suffering because of him. Instead, she concentrated her thoughts on Laurie's best friend. She wondered why Barbara would do such a thing to Laurie when they were like sisters. She found Barbara's action beyond greed and thought to herself that Barbara was an evil whore.

"Mom, it's already been a week and she never called, even though she knew you went to the emergency room that night."

"Well... That's the way the cookies crumble," Carlette added.

Carlette shared more advice with Laurie and told her about adversities in life. Laurie understood every single thing that her mother told her. Nevertheless, it was different for her. It was easier said than done.

Vicki did her best to help Laurie. Following the meeting in the boardroom, she tried to convince every other board member. However, none of them wanted to stand against Junior's decision. In the following days, she tried harder and even made phone calls to other companies. Unfortunately, all Vicki's networks said that they were not ready to handle the pressure from the media that Laurie carried with her. In addition, Laurie's presence could disturb their work environment. Many CEO's saw Laurie as a virus: a brand's destructor or human work infection. Many people acted like Laurie was the one who shot the gentleman.

Wherever Laurie went, paparazzi followed her. Many journalists insisted to interview her about her relationship with the bouncer. Every day they were standing in front of her building and waiting for her to step out. She refused to talk to any media because she was a quiet woman who liked her privacy. It was a nightmare for Laurie whenever she had to go somewhere. For her peace, Laurie went back to live in Michigan with her mother on August 8, 2012.

Laurie realized the impact of her voice mail when she got to the airport. When she landed in Michigan, nothing changed. People were able to recognize her. Everyone stared at her. It was embarrassing for her. Fortunately, she had her sunglasses that helped her avoid eye contact with anybody.

Carlette understood the pressure that her daughter had to deal with. She advised Laurie to not go out for a few weeks, hoping that people might forget about her. Sometimes, fame can become shame and makes earth feel like hell for someone.

Pen and Ink Edition was preparing its big move when doctors said the bouncer would be out in one week. Clair wanted to make a grand premiere with the book. She told the gentleman she scheduled the book's signing three days after his release from the hospital, an idea well-received by the gentleman. In the media, social media, buses, trains, taxis, and other places, anyone could see and read about the upcoming signing. The public was very excited about that news.

On August 9, the gentleman went back to his house five weeks after being admitted to *Santa Philomena Hospital*. He was happy to leave because he felt like he was in jail. The room was the cell and the IV connected to his arm was the handcuffs. He gave a short interview with two journalists and went home with Gabriel.

AUGUST 11, 2012

The gentleman had been signing books since 11:00 a.m. Many people came out for *Guilty of Natural Beauty* signing. They took pictures with him and the media was there as well. It was a big event. It was the first time a writer mobilized so many people in the United States for a book signing.

Around 2:15 p.m., the media focused on the gentleman who was giving a speech on his first novel. He also affirmed that he was working on his second book. Barbara came up front and made a request to the gentleman in public. He gave an affirmative answer to her.

That day, Anna came back from her vacation to Marseille and she became aware Carlette and Laurie were in Michigan. She visited them right away. Carlette was like a sister to Anna. She considered Laurie like her own daughter. Like everybody else, Anna saw the news about Barbara, Laurie, and the bouncer. But she believed nothing said in the media. She looked forward to meeting Laurie to ask her what really happened.

As soon as Anna walked in Carlette's house, she asked her friend for Laurie. Carlette was cooking dinner when Anna arrived. They chatted a little about the incident at the hospital and then Anna went to Laurie's room to talk to her.

Laurie was sitting down on her bed with her legs folded underneath her as she told Anna the conversation she had with Barbara that Saturday morning after the gentleman left. Anna leaned on a dresser that was in the room and listened to what Laurie said and analyzed the facts. Anna told Laurie that she should have listened to her heart instead of Barbara's comments. Yet it was so difficult for Laurie to accept her mistake. She said with an angry voice, "I knew he was a dog. He cheated on me. When I asked him if he was faithful and if I could trust him, he smiled and told me that I didn't have to think about. He's a liar."

"How did he cheat on you when he met Barbara before you and slept with her only once?" Anna asked.

"We went out a few times. Why didn't he mention anything about Barbara?" Laurie paused and complained, "Since the day I met him, troubles haven't stopped coming into my life."

"Sweetheart, don't be too emotional. Take your time and think more about it." Anna paused and then asked,

"You were only dating a month. Would you want to hear that? If you had slept with someone right before you met the gentleman, would you tell him?"

Laurie could not find an answer for these questions. She remained silent because she knew Anna hit the nail on the head. A few minutes later, Anna and Laurie joined Carlette in the kitchen for dinner. They both took seats at the kitchen table as Carlette served them. Laurie became nauseous right away from the smell of the roast beef. She made it to the bathroom just in time to vomit in the toilet bowl. Carlette and Anna ran after her to make sure she was okay. After throwing up, Laurie took a shower and then went to her bedroom to take a nap.

Carlette explained to Anna that since they came back to Michigan, all Laurie wanted to do was sleep. She did not have an appetite and only snacked on chips and sweets. Carlette explained that she thought it was due to stress or maybe the side effects of the sleeping pills that Laurie was taking. Anna gave a worried look to Carlette and then shook her head.

"I have a feeling she's pregnant. Should we buy her a pregnancy test? Just to be sure," Carlette asked.

"It's not a good idea. She's not a teen. We shouldn't interfere in her private life like that. Give her a few more days. I also wanna talk to him because I want to hear his version of the story," Anna answered.

"Laurie has his number. Ask her."

Anna nodded. "I'll do that before I leave."

Anna and Carlette whispered in the living room. They both thought they could convince the gentleman to forgive Laurie for her emotional action. They wanted to explain to him how much they loved him for Laurie and see how he could make it work. The television was already on when the news started.

"It's 7:00 o'clock. Let's watch the news," Carlette proposed.

Anna nodded and sat down on the couch with Carlette. They both paid attention to the news. A few minutes later, Anna stood up, and went back in the kitchen to drink some water. Before she even had time to pour the liquid into her glass, Carlette called out, "Anna, Anna..."

"Yes Carlette...."

"Come in here," Carlette said.

Anna hurried back into the living room. Carlette and her watched Barbara get on her knees, show a ring to the gentleman, and ask him, "Will you marry me?"

Barbara was quick and smart. She chose the perfect time to make her request. She knew the media and the crowd would play in her favor.

The gentleman was shocked. Asking for marriage was the last thing he would have expected from Barbara. He did not want to be rude. He knew that any mistake could ruin his career. The gentleman looked at Barbara, took her hand to raise her up, and said, "Yes, I will..."

Everyone present in the room cheered. Barbara kissed and hugged him. What a great play by Barbara. She looked at him and stated, "I am the happiest woman alive because of you. Finally God answered my prayer. I could no longer wait to be yours. You transformed my life and I want to be with you for the rest of my life."

"I'm honored by those words, and I hope I will be able to keep you happy."

The gentleman who was good at loving speech, but this time he kept it short and simple. He had his heart set on Laurie, but his pride made him accept Barbara's proposal. He knew so little about Barbara.

Anna could not believe what she watched on the television. She was so shocked that she dropped the cup of water on the carpet. The strength of her knees vanished. Anna sat down on the couch with her left hand in her mouth and stared at the television in disbelief.

At the same time, Laurie was entering the living room. She asked her mother wistfully, "Mom, do you think I should call him? I wanna talk to him before it's too late."

Carlette quickly turned off the TV when she heard her daughter's voice.

Both, Anna and Carlette, looked at Laurie and did not say a single word. Laurie thought that look from her mother and Anna meant that she was crazy. She sat down on the couch between her mother and Anna. She began to cry and confessed, "It's not easy to let go once you had a taste of a good thing. If only he could give me a chance to say that I am sorry. I will tell him how I feel when he is next to me. His arms carry such comfort that they can hold captive the heart of anyone who dares to approach him. I don't wanna lose him."

"Your mother and I experienced that same feeling when he hugged us," Anna said.

"He has a personality far beyond expectations. It's like he's happiness himself," Carlette added.

"I miss his funny jokes, his way of communicating, and everything about him. I want to be with that face that makes me dream, that smile that brings me happiness, that warm hug that comforts me and gives me peace," Laurie continued.

In those words, Anna and Carlette shed tears. Laurie's speech was like a knife that was piercing their hearts. The gentleman left his imprint on Laurie's heart.

That night was one of the most painful nights for both Anna and Carlette. They did not know if they should tell Laurie the truth about Barbara and the gentleman or let her find out on her own. Finally, they let the night pass and hoped sleep would bring them wisdom to manage such a delicate situation. They remained silent until Laurie went to sleep.

Anna called home to let her family know that she was staying with Carlette for the night. Carlette unfolded her couch and sat down on it with Anna. They both extended their legs and were immersed in deep thoughts until sleep caught them.

Around 10:00 p.m., Gabriel came home and went straight to his brother's room. He could not wait any longer.

I Dare You To Try It

The engagement of his brother to Barbara surprised him. He asked him, "What I heard on the news - is it true?"

"Yup."

Gabriel was more than confused with his brother's attitude than the answer. One moment, the gentleman was asking non-stop for the wolverine lady. All of the sudden, another woman claimed a pregnancy and the next step was an engagement. To Gabriel, the "Yup" answer sounded like someone forced his brother to marry Barbara or his brother would have given an emotional response. No matter what the case, Gabriel knew that the best thing to do was to question the gentleman about his engagement decision.

"So... What made you want to marry her?"

The gentleman was fixing his bed and did not bother to look at Gabriel. With a firm tone of voice, he answered, "She will be the mother of my child."

"How long have you been seeing her?"

"I saw her on a Thursday night at *Heaven*. We spent a couple of minutes together, then we went to her apartment, and we hooked up. The next thing I know she came to the hospital and said that she's pregnant."

"Do you think it's the best decision for you?"

The gentleman nodded.

"How do you know it's your child?" Gabriel paused and asked, "Do you love her?"

The gentleman could not answer these questions. Gabriel understood that his brother already made up his mind. He had to respect his choice and pray that everything went well. Gabriel patted his brother's left shoulder, and said, "Congratulations Bro," before he went to his room.

The gentleman took his favorite position on his bed. Half naked, wearing navy blue boxers, he lay on his bed with his hands behind his head like he was on a beach. He stared at the beige ceiling of his bedroom. The ceiling was like a big flat screen for him where he was reviewing all his acts, his success and failures especially of his last two conquests. He spent the entire night trying to figure out the reasons he gave a positive answer to Barbara's request and why did Laurie have such a negative attitude toward him. He wished to erase some of his acts. Unfortunately, the past of someone cannot be undone. He accepted a proposal from a woman he barely knew. He realized that he would marry Barbara not because he loved her, but because she said she was pregnant with his child. The gentleman always affirmed that he wanted to be there to raise his kids. He wanted to live together with his child and the mother of his kids. After deep thinking, he realized he sacrificed his happiness for his child's future.

AUGUST 12, 2012

Around 8:00 a.m., Anna and Carlette woke up. They heard that the TV in Laurie's room was tuned on. So they went upstairs to check on her. They saw she was watching the news about the engagement between Barbara and the gentleman. Anna and Carlette stood in each corner of the door and stared at Laurie. They could not find any words to say to her.

Laurie glanced at them and reassured them she would recover. Carlette went to sit down on the bed beside her daughter and Anna leaned on the dresser. A few minutes later, Laurie said, "I've would never imagined my life turning out like this. I've worked so hard. My future looked so bright. A simple foolish kiss was enough to destroy my dreams. I wished to have kids, but… not in this condition… raising a child without the father. Shame on me."

"Wait a minute, are you trying to say that you're pregnant?" Anna asked as she looked at Laurie.

"Yes, I am... unfortunately," Laurie answered regretfully.

"How do you know?" Anna asked.

"I woke up in the middle of the night and I was thinking about the way I've been feeling the past few days. I decided to run to the pharmacy that is open twenty-four hours on Josephine Street and buy a few pregnancy tests. When I came back, I took the test twice, and I had the same results. I'm definitely pregnant."

Anna glanced at Carlette and remained silent as she raised her chin to stare at the ceiling for a few seconds.

"Why didn't you tell us? We could have gone with you," Carlette said.

"I know mom, but I didn't want to bother you guys too much. And I figured it was the best time to go out since there were so few people in the street," Laurie added.

Anna and Carlette comforted Laurie. They promised to never give up on her and that they would help her. Anna said that it would be important to tell the gentleman that Laurie was pregnant by him. However, Carlette and her daughter did not want to go through that after suffering so much from the media. Laurie told them that the gentleman always talked about his brother. She said maybe they could contact Gabriel and tell him about the future baby.

That morning upon waking, the gentleman made up his mind. He understood his mistake and accepted his fate.

He remembered that his mother used to tell him that everything in life happened for a reason. His brother and him were born and raised in a Christian family. Their parents taught them to believe in God.

The gentleman left his room, went to the bathroom to brush his teeth, and then went in the kitchen. He saw a magnet on the door of the refrigerator that had been there for years. Yet he never read the saying, *"For each of his children, God has a plan."* He meditated on those words while preparing his breakfast. He used the Bible as reference to convince himself of everything that happened in his life. The gentleman realized that he was still alive despite being shot five times. The book of Psalms says, *"A righteous man may have many troubles, but the Lord delivers him from them all."*

In less than a month, he passed from struggle to wealth. His old boss Marc-Allan himself wanted to be his bodyguard. He remembered those days when the manager of *Team Undercover* used to yell at him like he was a child. Clair, who published his first book without advertising it because he was an unknown author, was now begging him to finish his second novel as soon as possible. The most successful literary agents in New York were harassing him with calls and emails. They were fighting to represent him. Some even offered their services for free for his second book. He believed that his meeting with Laurie was not a coincidence even though she departed his life too soon. Somehow, he thought things would be better with Barbara after their wedding. *"You prepare a table before me in the presence of my enemies. You anoint my head with oil; my cup overflows. Surely goodness and love will follow me all the days of my life."* Once he finished his breakfast, he bowed his head, thanked the Lord, and then took his pain and antibiotic medications.

The gentleman went in the living room and saw his brother watching the last day of the 2012 Summer Olympics in England. He had a short conversation with Gabriel about the records of different athletes. Then he sat down on the sofa and enjoyed the men's bronze medal basketball game with his brother. They both were passionate about basketball.

Five minutes later, the doorbell rang; Gabriel went to open the door and saw Barbara. She kissed him on his cheek and walked inside. She hugged her fiancé and gave him a warm kiss on his lips. The gentleman did not expect to see Barbara that morning. He did not like surprise visits. The gentleman wished she could have called or texted him that she was coming over. He gave her a wry smile and pretended he was happy to see her. Barbara sat down on the left corner of the sofa next to her fiancé and put her bag next to her.

"How are you doing?" the gentleman asked.

"Great my love, now I'm next to you," Barbara replied with a big smile and kissed the gentleman on his cheeks.

"How's everything?"

"So far so good. Sometimes, I have some discomfort, but it's okay. I guess that's normal for a pregnant woman," Barbara replied and then paid attention to the game between Russia and Argentina.

A few minutes later, Barbara started caressing her fiancé's head and neck and then said, "I've been searching on the Internet and I found some places for our wedding and the wedding party. I chose friends and family members of mine to be groomsmen and bridesmaids. I also contacted the priest."

"It seems like you've already done everything," the gentleman said.

"I hope you're not mad at me," Barbara teased.

The gentleman looked at Barbara and said, "No... That's good. You're a responsible person. I don't care who you chose for anything else, but I want Gabriel to be my best man. And I don't want a long ceremony."

Gabriel was shocked to hear his brother choose him as best man. Despite being so close with him, Gabriel would have never thought something like that because he was younger than his brother and he did not have any experience in marriage or in relationships. Gabriel glanced at his brother and smiled. It was a big honor for him.

"Well... of course, he's your brother. After all, it's up to the groom to choose his best man," Barbara added with a grin.

Barbara grabbed her IPad from her bag and started showing the gentleman different places where they could get married and different rings she would like to have. She also told him about the color she picked for the wedding. Even though she came with different options, her desire was go to St Francis Church on 12th Avenue and 62nd Street for the wedding ceremony and to rent a yacht for the party. She wanted her wedding to be early in the morning at 10:00 a.m. and by 1:00 p.m. she could already be enjoying the party with her friends. She also detailed every little thing that she wanted for that special occasion. The gentleman agreed with all her propositions.

Gabriel wondered why Barbara acted so rude. She did not even care if the gentleman was watching the basketball game. She wanted him to focus only on her and talk about their wedding. Gabriel watched the game until its end, but he did not say a word, and then he went to his bedroom and gave some privacy to his brother and Barbara.

Barbara spent almost three hours with the gentleman. However, she did not even pay attention to how he was doing. The entire time was dedicated to the wedding. Once she got his authorization, she kissed him, and went back to her apartment.

AUGUST 13, 2012

The next day, early in the morning, Anna left for New York City with the strong intent to meet with the gentleman. When she got off the plane, she took a taxi, and went to the address from the mail sent to Laurie by the gentleman. She arrived at her destination and rang the bell. A young handsome man in his early twenties wearing a blue t-shirt and black jeans opened the door. She looked at him and knew right away he was the gentleman's brother because he resembled him very much. Anna made a quick self-introduction and urgently requested to speak to the gentleman. Gabriel told her that his brother would be back around 8:30 p.m.

Gabriel saw the rush and worry that the woman carried. So he asked her if she would not mind to share with him the message and he would pass it along to his brother upon his return. Anna agreed to talk to him, and he invited her in.

Once Anna walked in, she glanced at the entire living room. She was surprised to see how clean and organized the small living room looked. She also saw two black and white photos of Gabriel and the gentleman when they were toddlers. Anna sat down on the sofa and then she explained to him the reason for her visit. It was one of those rare occasions where she had to do the talking instead of asking questions like she was used to.

Gabriel stared at Anna with confusion as he listened to her story. At first, he did not believe her, but he gave her the benefit of doubt based on her age and knowing also that his brother was in a relationship with Laurie. Gabriel wanted to protect his brother and discover the truth behind that pregnancy claimed by both Barbara and Laurie. Therefore, he promised Anna that he would help Laurie with the child and would visit her in Michigan as soon as he could.

Anna was satisfied with her trip following the promises made by the gentleman's brother. She talked to Gabriel for about forty minutes. And then, she took another taxi that drove her to a hotel close to JFK Airport called *Bon Sommeil Hotel* where she stayed for one night before her flight back to Michigan the next day.

Following that meeting with Anna, Gabriel started thinking about what to do if both women were pregnant by his brother at the same time. He hoped no more women came forward claiming to be pregnant by his brother. One thing was certain; Gabriel knew that his brother loved Laurie. The gentleman talked a lot about her until that Tuesday when Barbara showed up, and everything had shifted.

Gabriel did not have a chance to see Laurie face to face neither to interact with her, but so far, he did not like Barbara. He kept in contact with Anna over the phone. Three days later, he decided to visit Laurie. He planned for Anna to pick him up at the airport and bring him to Carlette's house.

AUGUST 16, 2012

Gabriel left his house around 11:00 a.m. and went to LaGuardia Airport. He carried a gym bag that contained his laptop, one camera, and some of his clothes. He was so passionate about photography that he carried a camera wherever he went. As soon as the pilot announced that they would land in Michigan in thirty minutes, some scary thoughts came into Gabriel's mind.

He wondered if he had gone too far in his goal to discover the truth because he decided to go all the way to Michigan by himself. And nobody else knew where he was going. He told his brother he was going upstate New York for film training. Gabriel wondered if it was a trap and these people planned to harm him after what happened between his brother and Laurie. He knew that the United States was a well-defended country, but that its citizens were capable of doing crazy things. The closer he got to the airport, the more afraid he became.

When Gabriel left the airport, Anna was already outside waiting for him. As soon as he got to Anna's car, his heart started pounding. She asked him about the trip and if he had said anything to his brother by chance. Gabriel told her that all his family, except his brother, was well aware of his trip to Michigan. As they drove, Anna asked him questions about his career, his preferences, and if he was not seeing any girl at that moment. Gabriel managed to have a decent conversation with Anna. Nevertheless, his voice was unbalanced. His blood pressure rose when he got out the car and was about to enter the house. He managed to not show any signs of stress or fear. However, he kept his phone in his hand, ready to dial 911 if anything went bad.

Gabriel presented himself to the family and listened to the story. Carlette explained to Gabriel how difficult it was for her daughter to get her life back, especially with those journalists who did not stop harassing her daughter. She begged him to keep his visit and the news about Laurie's pregnancy a secret to everybody including his brother.

After listening to all three women, Gabriel offered his financial support to the family. Laurie refused his help, but Anna and Carlette tried to convince her to accept because they said that the gentleman would know nothing about that.

Laurie agreed under one condition: she would only accept a visit from Gabriel and nothing else.

Following the meeting, Gabriel wanted to go to a hotel to spend the rest of the day. Carlette offered that he stay with them because there was another room available in the house. Carlette owned a two-floor ranch home with four bedrooms. Gabriel accepted the offer to stay at the Lugbowskovsky home for the night because their hospitality was beyond his expectations. The care they showed him was natural. Anyone who visited the Lugbowskovsky family always praised their hospitality and generosity.

Carlette changed the sheets on the bed and then showed him the room where he was staying at for the night. She also gave him a quick tour of the house noting where the kitchen and the bathroom were.

Before Anna went to her house, she asked Gabriel about the time of his flight departure for New York and told him she would drive him back to the airport. He accepted her offer.

After diner, Carlette washed the dishes, took a shower, and went to bed. Meanwhile, in the living room Laurie and Gabriel had a little conversation in which they tried to get to know each other a little before they went to bed. She made him feel like he was her brother; something he really appreciated. Gabriel maintained a broad conversation with Laurie. Most of the time they spent was dedicated to soccer; a subject he was more than happy to discuss. He was surprised to see that Laurie knew a lot about the major soccer leagues around the world. Around 10:00 p.m., Laurie went upstairs to her room and Gabriel to his.

Before he slept, the scary thoughts came back to his mind. He tried to shove them away. Gabriel realized that Carlette and Laurie did not look dangerous after all. However, he chose to be cautious and watchful. He looked around the room to see how someone could enter. The room had two doors; he locked both of them and then quietly blocked one door with the bed and the other one with a dresser that was in the room. Gabriel made sure that nobody could get in. He kneeled to pray before he slept.

The next morning, Gabriel woke up and put everything back in place and then took a shower. Carlette was already awake and was making pancakes in the kitchen. He greeted her and went into the living room. He sat down on the big fluffy light brown sofa and glanced over the brick wall, the coffee table, the fireplace, and the TV on a stand as he was waiting for Anna. The decor made anyone feel at home.

A few minutes later, Carlette called him and asked him what he wanted to eat before he left. Gabriel walked into the traditional country style kitchen with brown tiles and cherry wood furniture. He took a banana, two pancakes, an apple, and some orange juice. The pancakes did not only smell good, but they were delicious.

Gabriel loved the cooking skills that Carlette possessed. He had not received that much attention and tasted great food like that since his mother passed away. Carlette told him to take more pancakes. He refused her politely because he had to show manners when he was with a stranger, but deep inside he wanted to eat more.

Gabriel was about to leave when Laurie came downstairs. She hugged him and wished him a safe trip. Anna picked him up on time and drove him to the airport. On his way back, Gabriel thought a lot about the food especially the pasta with veggies they had for dinner the night before and the warm welcome he received. The kindness of the Lugbowskovsky family made him want to return to Michigan as soon as possible. For a moment, he forgot he was on a mission.

Following that visit to Michigan, Laurie had an advantage over Barbara on the race in Gabriel's mind. As a brother and selected best man, Gabriel wanted his brother to make the best choice — marry the woman who could make him happy. His biggest concern was finding proof of pregnancy for both Barbara and Laurie.

Barbara continued to plan her wedding and visit her fiancé. She was still working at the accounting firm. The gentleman was working on another novel and going to rehab at *Santa Philomena Hospital* every two days. Meanwhile, Gabriel was working as a detective. He was observing Barbara's attitude and kept questioning the gentleman about his feelings for Barbara and Laurie.

AUGUST 24, 2012

Laurie and Gabriel became more open to each other. On his third trip to Michigan, he asked Laurie some key questions. They were sitting in the back yard of the house. The sun was almost gone, and the stars were showing in the sky. They were having a casual conversation when Gabriel asked, "Why don't you want him to know that you're also pregnant?"

"I don't want to disturb his life. He's engaged now. She's also pregnant. In addition, she met him before I did," Laurie answered in sorrow.

"I understand, but he has to know. He could take care of the child."

"Honestly, I accepted your visit because I wanted you to know about the child. It wasn't about money. The mistake was mine. I will find a way to take care of my baby, but I hope you will continue to visit us," Laurie said with a shaky tone of voice.

"I'm sorry, but it's not what I mean. If it was me, I would want to know. Maybe I could make a better choice."

Gabriel thought if Laurie told the gentleman about her pregnancy, his brother would change his mind about marrying Barbara. He saw that his brother was not happy with Barbara. For a moment they remained silent; Laurie stared at the sky and Gabriel glanced over every flower pot in the backyard. A few minutes later, he looked at Laurie and asked, "What do you think about Barbara? She was your friend, wasn't she?"

"Before I could tell, but now I can't."

He nodded and then asked, "Why did you move to New York?"

"Barbara and I were like sisters. We were always together. She moved to New York in May 2008. She always told me to move in with her, but I was reluctant. I loved Michigan so much and I couldn't picture myself living somewhere else. Three months later, I visited her in New York. We went out on a Wednesday night and we met a guy named Wilson Mikelis. He was cool. We chatted a little bit, and he told us he was recruiting sales people for a pharmaceutical company. Wilson offered me a job and gave me his business card. Barbara told me to not miss out on the opportunity. The following day, I went for an interview and lucky me... I got hired."

"Wow... That was wonderful."

Laurie smiled at him and continued, "I was doing pretty well as saleswoman and Wilson always advised me to go for a Master's in marketing. Finally, I went for the Master's degree and I was hired at *Pelito & Co* two weeks after my graduation. Barbara and I lived together until she met James and moved to another apartment with him before they got married."

Gabriel looked at Laurie in confusion when he heard: *before they got married.* Laurie understood his concern and rephrased her last sentence, "I mean they were supposed to get married."

"What happened between James and her?"

"I don't know... They looked pretty much in love. Two weeks before the wedding, James called it off and then, he disappeared."

"Why?"

"I have no idea." Laurie shrugged.

"Hmm..."

"You will see the true nature of people when money is involved. She advised me to stop seeing your brother because he was a bouncer, but she was the first to come up front and propose marriage to him because your brother is a millionaire now. I'm not mad at her because she met him before me. I was too emotional, and she did what she had to do. I hope she will be good to him and make him happy."

"What do you mean by she did what she had to do?"

Laurie sighed and answered, "She wanted him, and she fought for him. While I love him, but ran away." She paused and then asked him, "How's your relationship with her?"

"Mmm... the only thing that matters to her is her wedding. She's so into it. Can I ask you a personal question? I mean very personal if you don't mind?"

"Sure, sure... why not?" Laurie answered hesitantly.

"Can you tell me a little about my brother? If you don't mind."

Laurie sighed following that interesting question, "Oh boy! That's a tough question."

"It's okay if you don't wanna say anything."

Laurie glanced at him, smiled, and said, "I'm passionate about the look he gave me. He melted my heart with his words and text messages. His eyes are magic. I can't resist him. Your brother is the first man who truly gave me a reason to dream about love. And he's cool. He likes to joke and he's funny too."

Laurie was very personal; however, when it came to describing the gentleman, she was not ashamed to do it. Laurie paused, took a deep breath, and continued, "I become lovesick once I think about him. The warmth of his lips on my cheek, the softness of his touch on my skin, his kindness, and everything.... I would say that the fire of his love consumed me, I dream of him each night. Your brother is my obsession."

"Wow," Gabriel added as he saw tears filling her eyes.

Gabriel looked at her facial expression. He could tell that her words came from her heart and she spoke the truth. He knew that any woman who was in love with his brother, talked about the gentleman's eyes, lips, and jokes. His brother used almost the same words when he asked him questions about Laurie. Gabriel was convinced about the love shared between his brother and Laurie.

"I hope you'll keep my confession a secret. So... What do you know about me?" Laurie asked as she managed to not let any tears fall down her cheeks.

"Well... At the beginning, I didn't know your name. I always asked him for the wolverine lady," Gabriel said with a grin.

"Why wolverine lady?" Laurie asked with a smile.

Gabriel smiled, shook his head, and said, "One Saturday morning, he came home and following a shower, he asked me to look at his back. I saw nail traces on it and I told him he was fighting a female version of wolverine. After the incident, I knew your real name in the media, but my brother keeps using wolverine lady when he's talking about you."

"So you're the one who gave me that nickname?"

"Yeah, pretty much."

Laurie smiled at Gabriel and said, "You're like him. He always makes me smile. I miss him and his jokes about that Joe. Please I beg you do not say anything to your brother."

"I won't. And if there's anything you need, please let me know."

"Thanks a lot, I really appreciate that. Your presence, that's what really matters."

"You're welcome. You're part of the family."

Laurie felt opened enough to acknowledge her mistake and explain to him the reason for her emotional voicemail to Barbara. Laurie and Gabriel continued their dialogue before they went back inside and ate dinner. That night, Carlette made penne with vodka, another one of her specialties. They watched a comedy movie together before they all went to sleep.

The following day, early in the morning, Anna drove Gabriel to the airport. They talked about the difference in lifestyles and neighborhoods in both Michigan and New York. When she was almost at the airport, she said to him, "I heard people say you grew up in a tough neighborhood. I'm surprised that your environment did not influence you. You managed to stay focused on your goals. You're such a good person. Even though I've only known you for a little, I'm proud of you."

"Thanks," Gabriel replied.

"Are you still living in the same neighborhood?"

"Yes, we are."

Anna was surprised that Gabriel and his brother had not yet moved. She shrugged and then said, "I'm happy that you come so often to Michigan. It's such a big relief for both Laurie and Carlette. Thanks a lot."

"Don't thank me. I'm doing my family duties."

Gabriel was more muscular, but shorter than his brother. He had a beard and was always serious and projected a look of more maturity than the baby face of the gentleman and his joking skills. Anna was the first to pick the gentleman for Laurie, but also she was also the first to lose faith and said, "I wished it was you Laurie met that Friday night."

"Mmm... You don't know my brother. He's a man with great heart and I can't even walk in his shadow," Gabriel said as he looked at Anna.

"If you say so... The future will tell the rest."

Anna dropped him at the airport, hugged him, and wished him a safe trip. He told her he would come back the following weekend. Gabriel was thinking about a way to help Laurie since she did not want money from him nor his brother. Before landing in New York, he found a solution.

To his big surprise, a wedding card was waiting for Gabriel at home. Barbara already printed the wedding invitation cards and started giving them out. He understood that it was too late to convince his brother to make a U-turn on that project. Laurie texted him and told him she heard about the gentleman's wedding date on the news. Gabriel replied that he just received the news and his brother selected him to be the best man. That day Laurie became desperate and realized that it was over for her.

Barbara came to the gentleman's house almost every day to discuss the same subject. Whenever she came in, Gabriel stepped out. He did not want to interact with her. However, he continued to visit Laurie in Michigan.

AUGUST 29, 2012

That Wednesday, around 4:30 p.m., Gabriel was watching a Champions League play-off second-leg game with his brother, and Barbara stopped by. She kissed him and her fiancé. Right away, she started talking about the wedding. Gabriel found her so annoying with all the wedding talk. Five minutes later, he stood up and said,

"Gotta go. I got some stuff to take care of."

The gentleman looked at his brother and was shocked to see him leaving in the middle of a game between S.C Braga from Portugal and Udinese Calcio from Italy. He knew Gabriel was excited about that matchup. Both teams were heading to extra time, and Gabriel was passionate about penalty stage.

"Don't you want to help me with my wedding?" Barbara asked.

"I'm pretty sure you'll take care of everything," Gabriel answered with a firm tone of voice.

"What kind of best man are you?" Barbara demanded.

"The one who would save the groom from disaster."

"What?" Barbara said in confusion.

She received no answer for that question because Gabriel closed the door behind him. Then she turned her head toward her fiancé and said, "Your brother is weird." The gentleman shook his head, smirked, and replied, "He's a quiet guy, but he's cool."

Four hours later, Gabriel came back home. He thought Barbara would have left, but she had not. He crossed the living room, but before he got into his room, the gentleman said, "Hey, do you have time to help us with the wedding planning?

Since Gabriel was certain about Laurie, he took the opportunity to express his feelings on the marriage. Gabriel tried to convince his brother to think again on his decision by questioning him.

"What if Barbara was not pregnant, but Laurie was? Or… if both were pregnant, what would you do?"

"If Laurie was she would have told me," the gentleman answered with a firm tone of voice.

"Maybe you didn't give her that opportunity. And why did you pick your fiancé over her?" Gabriel insisted.

"After saving her life, she thanked me with ingratitude. I'll be a father soon and you know where I stand in this matter," the gentleman growled.

Tension escalated between the brothers and Barbara watched them argue. She did not even try to calm them down. Gabriel wanted his brother to rethink his marriage to Barbara. Since he promised Laurie to keep her secret safe, he did not speak clearly, but hoped that his brother would change his mind.

"What has come over you? All of the sudden, you talk like you are my father or older than I without respect."

"You chose me as your best man, so I'm playing my role."

Gabriel turned his head and walked toward his room. Before he even took five steps forward, he turned around, looked at his brother and asked, "Did you understand why Laurie said those things about you. Did you really know the truth about everything?"

"I was in the hospital for five weeks... five weeks... She never visited me or texted me, or called me once. Not even once... Of course, I received flowers and cards under her mother's name. Can you give me an answer for that, Mr. Best man?" the gentleman replied in fury.

"I can't convince you. Just... Good luck man."

"What is your problem? Why don't you want this marriage?" Barbara asked.

Gabriel looked Barbara straight in the eyes and said, "To be honest with you, Barbara, I don't like that everything is being rushed. It doesn't feel right. I would stop it if I could." Then he walked in his room and locked the door behind him.

Gabriel's comments had angered the gentleman. He shook his head and compressed his lips. His fiancé stared at him like she was asking him if he was not going to talk to his little brother.

"Don't even ask me about his attitude," the gentleman snapped.

Five minutes later, Barbara grabbed her belongings, kissed the gentleman and walked out. She got into her car and threw her bag in fury in the back seat. Once she reached her apartment, she wondered why Gabriel had acted so weird since the beginning. She kept replaying Gabriel's last sentence in her mind, *"I would stop it if I could."* She has been dreaming about marrying a rich man for so long, and she was so close to making her dream come true.

Barbara realized that Gabriel represented a big threat to her goal. Taking Gabriel out of the equation became her obsession. She was ready to do anything to marry the gentleman. She believed there was no way that Gabriel could stop her from being the wife of his brother. Since that day, tension rose between Barbara and Gabriel. A cold war began.

Barbara was raised by her father, an alcoholic who worked in a pizzeria his entire life. He was so talented that he could have owned his own pizza place, but he was not a risk taker. He preferred to serve instead of being served.

Even at home, he always avoided his reality and responsibilities. Fortunately, Barbara's mother and Carlette were good friends. Her mother died when she was six years old, and the Lugbowskovsky family was always kind to Barbara. They always included her on holidays.

Barbara did not have the best childhood. She was not used to gifts and vacations. Her favorite food was pasta and pizza because it was what her father could bring home from his work. She hated her father so much that she swore to never be in a relationship with a broke man. She was smart and focused in school. Once she moved to New York, she abandoned her father — not even a call once a year. Laurie tried in vain to convince her to forgive her father, but Barbara swore she'd rather die than talk to him.

Barbara was a winner with great character. She never gave up on any project she undertook. At school, at work, she never lost. She came across many rich men, yet she never caught any in her net because she was never taught how to win a man's heart. She believed her eloquence, achievement, and intelligence were enough to make every man fall for her. However, she had no concept of charm, sensitivity, patience or affection that men were looking for in a woman.

The next morning, Barbara woke up with her mind racing. She realized that despite the ring and the promise of marriage, something paramount was missing in all her victories. Besides the threat represented by Gabriel for her dream to marry a rich man, she knew that the gentleman's heart was not won yet. She wondered if it was the shooting that changed him or the traces of Laurie in his heart.

Barbara also knew that great people were not enough to win a war, but that they needed great strategy and tactic. So she went online to search for articles about love and relationships. Every day after work, she spent at least three hours reading articles and books online. She was committed to her goal. She wanted to make sure that she secured her upcoming wedding and captured her fiancé's heart. Even though she came across great information, she was not satisfied.

SEPTEMBER 7, 2012

On Friday after work, Barbara took the 1 train from 59th Street-Columbus Circle, got off on 28th Street and 7th Avenue, and went into a bookstore. When she entered the bookstore, she glanced at many books, but one captured her attention. She picked it up, read its introduction and conclusion, and then she bought it. The book was called: *Man vs. Woman, The Playbook*. The author used set plays in different sports to explain the relationship between men and women. Barbara started reading it as soon as she took a seat on the D train. She found the chapters interesting and informative.

The title of chapter 9 was: *Capture his mind with good sex and his heart will follow.* In that chapter, the author explained that men loved hookers because these women did things that normal women don't do. Also hookers always bring sexual creativity with a more open mind. The author also stated that the first need of a man is sex. Meanwhile for woman, it is love, affection, and attention. Barbara meditated a lot on chapter 9.

The next morning, she woke up, took a shower, and went to her fiancé's house. She wore a short button down black skirt dress with the belt tight at her waist, and the buttons unbuttoned enough to expose her cleavage. Barbara looked sexy that morning. She bought him coffee.

The gentleman was working on his laptop when he heard the doorbell ring. He walked toward the door and opened it for Barbara who greeted him with a kiss. Once she came in the house, she gave him the coffee, and sat down on the sofa. She came without her IPad and asked him questions about his recovery and other subjects. The gentleman forced a smile during his conversation with Barbara. Right after the gentleman finished his coffee; Barbara laid on the sofa, crossed her legs, and put her head on his lap. A few minutes later, she looked at him and asked, "Since our first meeting, you never had sex with me. Why?"

"We'll be married soon and we'll have plenty of time in front of us. I have to take it slow during my recovery."

"Hmmm…" she said as she shook her head and smiled.

"Also I wanna get certain things done and clear my mind a bit to perform well in the bed. You're carrying a baby so I want to take it slow and wait."

She sighed and said, "All right."

The gentleman looked disturbed. Barbara wanted to know what was going on his mind. She could have just asked him. Instead, she slipped her right hand under his t-shirt and caressed his chest. Barbara's caresses were pulling him away from his concerned world and bringing him back to her. A few minutes later, she raised her chin to look at him and said, "I feel like something is bothering you."

"Not really," he replied.

"Are you sure? Your face looks concerned."

"Really..." he answered while sighing and forced a fake smile.

"Are you excited or nervous about the wedding?"

"No, not at all. Women are more excited about marriage than men," he stated.

"True. Soon your heart will be filled with excitement. Only God knows how much you invade my heart with your caress. You're the most precious gift I've ever had."

The sweetness of Barbara's caress began to take all his frustration away. The gentleman stared at Barbara with his lips compressed. He realized there was something new; her demeanor had changed. For the first time, Barbara came to his house and asked him questions about his feelings without saying anything about the wedding. First, he shook his head and then, smiled at her.

"What..." Barbara asked with a smile.

"Nothing," the gentleman answered as he continued to smile.

They both laughed out loud. Barbara felt that the tactics in the book worked. It was the first time they shared a lovely and romantic smile. That romantic smile was followed by a sweet kiss. He knew that Barbara did not possess Laurie's divine smile. He realized that he should appreciate Barbara and get to know her better instead of expecting her to be like Laurie. A couple of minutes later, he asked, "Do you wanna play cards?"

"Yes, I do," she answered with delight.

The gentleman stood up and picked up the cards that were on the small living room table. They played under one rule: the loser kisses the winner. A few minutes later, Barbara lifted her left foot on the sofa, as she remained seated. The gentleman saw her red panties. He tried to focus on the game, but he could not stop glancing between her legs. Meanwhile, Barbara kept opening and closing her legs and acted like she was not aware that he was looking under her dress.

The more he fought not to glance at Barbara's panties the more his heart pounded. And his desire to have sex with her right on the sofa increased. Barbara saw that her fiancé sighed and his penis going up and down as it was imitating the beat of his heart. She believed that in the following minutes, he would be between her legs.

They were having a good time until they heard the keys in the door and saw the face of Gabriel. The gentleman's face changed right away and stared at his brother crossing the living room. Barbara muttered, "Fuck."

She was so close to her goal of having sex with her fiancé. She felt that Gabriel was a nightmare for her, but she managed to not show her anger because she knew how much the gentleman loved Gabriel.

Barbara was thinking about asking her fiancé to go in his room and continue the game. But once Gabriel came in the house, the gentleman followed him to his room. They started arguing. Barbara understood something was wrong between the brothers. She got up from the sofa and stood right outside of Gabriel's door. She listened to the conversation between the brothers. Barbara became aware that Gabriel was wasting the gentleman's money.

Barbara heard the bell ring and went to open the door. She saw Samuel who walked in and asked for the gentleman. She indicated with her finger that her fiancé was in the room with Gabriel. Samuel took a seat in the living room as he was waiting for his cousins.

The discussion escalated. The brothers argued so loud that it seemed they were about to fight. Samuel ran into the room and tried to calm the brothers down. Samuel stepped out of the house with the gentleman who complained about massive withdrawals made on his bank account by Gabriel.

Gabriel went to sit down on the sofa. Barbara was already thinking how she could break them apart. She knew Gabriel's presence next to his brother would jeopardize her wedding. She seized the occasion to throw blame and said what she hadn't been able to say to Gabriel. Barbara lost control and talked to Gabriel by pointing her right index finger at him, demanding, "What the fuck are you doing? You're a thief. You're a bastard and a jerk. Now I see why you don't want us to be married. You want him to stay here so you can steal every single penny he worked for. You're a waste."

Despite all she said, Gabriel remained silent. She continued to curse him out and kept coming close to him. Barbara stood right in front of Gabriel, bent over and yelled, "What kind of brother are you?" She paused, staring at him as she was waiting for an answer. Tired of his silence, Barbara snapped, "Asshole!" as she hit Gabriel with her index finger on his forehead.

Gabriel could not tolerate such an action by Barbara. He did not like her and she had the guts to not only curse him, but also hit him in the face. He pushed her back. She fell on the floor after her back hit the living room table and broke it.

The gentleman was coming back into the living room when he saw Gabriel push Barbara. He ran and punched Gabriel in the face many times before Samuel was able to grab him and stop the fight. Barbara stayed on the floor and moaned. The gentleman helped her stand before he put her on the sofa. Gabriel leaned on the wall and watched Barbara moaning in pain. He felt she deserved worse than that for her insolence.

Barbara held her back as she writhed in pain. The gentleman insisted that she go to the hospital to get checked out, but she refused. As soon as her back pain decreased, Barbara stood up, grabbed her purse, and left the house in tears. From that moment on, Gabriel and his brother stopped talking to each other. The gentleman had to take painkillers following his unexpected movement.

Samuel did not want any additional altercation between the brothers, so he advised Gabriel to go to a hotel and spend the night. Gabriel listened to his cousin who drove him to a motel on Flatlands. Before sleeping, Gabriel checked his face in the mirror. He saw that he had some cuts on his upper lip. He could have fought back, but he loved his brother so much and knew that he was not healed yet.

That night, Gabriel called Laurie and asked her if she would mind his presence at her mother's house for a few days. Laurie told him that it was fine with her. However, she would ask her mother. Fifteen minutes later, Laurie called Gabriel back and told him that her mother would be pleased to have him stay for a few days at their home.

The next morning, he took a cab and went back home before noon. The gentleman was watching a movie when Gabriel walked in. He did not say a word to him. He went straight to his room and locked the door behind him.

Three hours later, Gabriel walked out with his gym bag. He left a note on the kitchen table for his brother in which he told the gentleman that he decided to go out of state for a few days. The gentleman was sleeping when his little brother left. Upon his waking, he became aware of the note. Since he was angry, he did not mind that his brother would be gone for a few days.

During his flight, Gabriel was already dreaming about the dishes that Carlette made. Also, he would not have to see Barbara for a couple of days. He also thought it would be a great opportunity for him to visit different places in Michigan. Instead of asking Anna to pick him up at the airport, he took a taxi and went to the Lugbowskovsky's house. Upon his arrival, Laurie asked him, "What happened to your face?"

"It's nothing, I'm fine," he replied with a smile.

"Tell me what happened?" Laurie insisted.

Gabriel fabricated a quick story to explain the cuts on his face. "I was playing basketball and I was about to get the rebound when some guy elbowed me in the face by accident."

"Did you go to the hospital?"

"No... It's not that bad."

Laurie touched the small bump on his lip and he grimaced. Carlette went to the bathroom and brought him some painkillers and anti-inflammatory pills. By around 7:30pm, dinner was ready. Carlette made chicken Parmesan served over linguini.

SEPTEMBER 11, 2012

Three days following the fight between the brothers, Barbara called her fiancé. He was working on his new book when he picked up the call. The first thing he heard was Barbara mumbling words with her voice in distress.

"Hello... Hello... Are you okay, Barbara?" the gentleman asked.

"Please come here," Barbara cried.

"Where are you?"

"At my house," Barbara replied and then hung up.

The gentleman panicked and rushed to Barbara's house. He wondered what made her cry like that. Barbara lived at 110 West 12 Street Apt B8. The gentleman sprinted up the stairs as soon as Barbara buzzed him in. Once she opened her door, she leaned on him in desolation, and was crying hysterically. He wrapped her into his arms, rubbed her back, and tried to comfort her by shushing her. The gentleman continued to ask her why she was in tears, but she never answered him. Instead, she cried louder.

A few minutes later, she raised her chin, gave him a sheet of paper, and stated, "My doctor said I lost the child. Your brother reached his goal."

"What?" He called out in confusion and started to read the letter she handed him as he edged away from her.

The gentleman stared at his fiancé with his mouth open, but no words could come out. He wondered what kind of speech he should have in that moment to help her recover from her loss. The gentleman was also concerned about the reasons she had that miscarriage.

"Did the doctor tell you why you lost the baby?"

"When I left your house, I was in pain, but I was able to sleep. When I woke up yesterday I was bleeding. So I ran to the clinic, the doctor had me take some tests. This morning, I received a call from the clinic — doctor requested I come in immediately. When I got there he gave me the bad news. He explained that the shock I received on my waist when I fell on the table caused my loss. He told me that there was no way for them to save the fetus," Barbara explained to him as she leaned on the entrance door.

Everybody knows that a pregnant woman is fragile, and the gentleman witnessed how her fall on the table. Therefore, Barbara's tears on her cheeks and the letter from the doctor were enough to convince him the baby was gone. She also showed him her waist that was still red and swollen. He shook his head, sighed, and then called out, "Damn it." Definitely the date, September 11, was still haunting some people in the United States of America.

Barbara wanted her revenge and her best weapon was to turn her fiancé against Gabriel. She used her eloquence to convince the gentleman and pushed him to act quickly. Barbara edged toward him a couple of feet and pleaded, "He wasted not only your money, he's trying to ruin your life, your future. We lost our child… I know Gabe is your brother, but you have to do something before it's too late."

He wiped his hand over his distraught face and sighed. Then, he sat down on her couch and wondered how he got into this situation. He gritted his teeth and knew that he had to make a decision. A few minutes later, he stood up, walked towards his fiancé, and said, "I'm sorry babe. Please don't cry."

Barbara looked at him and answered him with questions, "How can I stop crying when I lost my baby? Do you know how painful it is for me? And the worst, you won't marry me because I'm not with child anymore," as more tears rolled down were falling on her cheeks.

The gentleman moved closer to her, with his arms opened, and tried to take her in his embrace. She weakly punched him on his chest with both hands and she called out in despair, "It's not fair… it's not fair…" as she continued to cry.

The gentleman knew it was a bitter experience for her. He tried to encourage her, "I understand, but that doesn't mean you will never have a baby." He held her in his embrace and continued, "Don't worry. We're not cancelling our wedding. And we will have another chance to try for another baby."

Barbara raised her chin to look at him and asked, "Are you serious?"

"Yes I am. And I also think it would be better if I move in with you. I'm going home to pack my clothes today and I will stay with you until our wedding," he reassured her with a gentle tone of voice and then he kissed her head affectionately. The gentleman took her hands and went to sit down on the couch with her. She leaned on him and he caressed her hair.

A few minutes later, Barbara asked, "Do you want me to hire a broker to find us a new apartment in Manhattan? My apartment is too small."

He nodded and replied, "Do it."

Barbara kissed the gentleman and fell asleep on his chest a few minutes later. The gentleman was so angry that he called his brother and told him he had chosen Samuel instead to be the best man for his wedding. As soon as Barbara fell asleep, the gentleman went to his house, grabbed some of his clothes and belongings, and came back to her apartment.

The following day, Barbara was bending on the floor and was looking for something beneath her couch as he was going to the bathroom. The gentleman glanced at the living room and saw her bending down. She wore a pink see-through lace thong with one of his white shirts, and rolled the sleeves.

For an instant, he gazed down at her behind and explored her slender waist and curvy body moving as she was trying to reach what she was looking for. The gentleman became more attracted to her. He rubbed his chin and fantasized in his mind the scene he could have made with her in such a position. He would kneel right behind her and slide one hand into her panty to move it to the side so he could have enough space to penetrate her, and then he would grab her hair into a ponytail. He would ride her, slap and bite her ass, and would enjoy the sound of her loud moan under his sway. Barbara said one truth about him; he was made for sex. His ability to create, innovate, and bring marvelous pleasure to any woman he slept with made him addictive. After finding what she was looking for and was about to stand up, the gentleman swallowed his desire and walked toward the bathroom to brush his teeth and shower.

During breakfast, the gentleman told his fiancée about the change he had made for the wedding regarding the best man. He also agreed to go shopping with her for the wedding that afternoon. When Barbara was showering, she smiled mischievously at the news of Gabriel being replaced by Samuel. She was proud and happy that the gentleman decided to live with her. In her mind, she realized it was not that hard to break the brothers apart.

They left the house around 2:15 p.m. Barbara could have driven to spare him the ninety-eight degrees outside, but instead she took a cab with him. She was so proud to hold his hand while entering stores. It was the first time they went out together and walked hand in hand. It was a great occasion for her to show off. She wore blue jeans, an off-the-shoulder white shirt, two gold bracelets on her right hand, and a gold necklace. She put on lace up leather peep toe booties in black, blue, and red. The gentleman had a slim fit khaki chino, a white shirt with sleeves rolled up, unbuttoned at the top with his dog tag, brown moccasins, and a nice watch.

Upon their return, the gentleman found the day exhausting. Not only did he have to deal with fans that asked him for signatures and taking photos with him, the media was also harassing him. The worst part was when Barbara entered a store; she looked at every single item like she wanted to buy everything. Even though he complained to her, she did the same thing in the next store she walked in. It was time consuming. He was not mad at her because he knew pretty well it was a female demeanor. Nevertheless, he did his best to keep a smile on his face during the outing. One thing was sure; he did not want to go for another shopping day.

They were on the bed and ready to sleep. Before they did, he said, "Barbie, I have to work on my second book and I need time. So, I won't be able to go everywhere with you."

I Dare You To Try It

For Barbara, the less the gentleman was involved, the more she needed to pay out of her pocket, and her choices cost an arm and a leg. She asked, "So you're telling me that your second book is more important than our wedding."

The gentleman sighed and shook his head. "It's not what I mean Barbie. I…"

Barbara rolled on him and kissed him before he even finished his sentence. That nickname gave her butterflies. She stated with an innocent voice, "I need you to pay off certain bills, babe. I can't afford everything. You know the day is approaching, and you've already agreed on certain things, right?"

The gentleman nodded and said, "I think it would be better if I go to the bank with you and give you access to my checking account. I will ask them for a book of checks so you can continue the planning. Women are better at wedding planning than men."

Barbara agreed to his proposition and kissed him. She felt the secrets from the book worked, and she was applying them meticulously. To seal the deal, she gave him a blowjob and made him jerk off before they slept.

The next morning, they both went to the bank and completed the paperwork. The gentleman gave Barbara full access to his checking account. She advised him to take Gabriel's signature off the account. He listened to her and replaced his brother's access with Barbara's. From now on, Barbara was able to continue the wedding project financially, and the gentleman had more time to focus on his new book.

SEPTEMBER 26, 2012

Eighteen days after the fighting, the gentleman decided to call his little brother because he had not heard from him since their argument. Despite everything that had happened, he loved him very much. Sometimes, a distance can teach someone how important the presence of somebody else in one's life. Gabriel was not only his little brother; he was also the gentleman's best friend.

Gabriel was taking a shower when his phone rang. He saw that the call was from his brother. He picked up the phone, put it on speaker since his body was wet, and because there was nobody else in the house at that moment. Carlette went out for food shopping and Laurie was at the clinic.

"What's up man?" the gentleman asked.

"Nothing. Chilling," Gabriel replied with a cold tone of voice.

Laurie came back earlier than expected. She walked in the house and was about to use the restroom when she heard the gentleman's voice on the phone. She walked closer to the door of the bathroom without making any noise and listened to the conversation.

"What have you been up to?" the gentleman asked.

"Nothing serious. How about you?"

"Same shit. Just working on a new project."

"Good."

"Can we talk a little?" the gentleman asked.

"Yeah man, go ahead."

"I'm, hmm... I'm sorry for what happened between us."

"It's okay," Gabriel said as he continued to respond to his brother with short answers.

Gabriel was upset because the only brother he had, the one he considered as a father, was able to drop him so fast for a woman. He would have never imagined someone could break him and the gentleman apart. That day when the gentleman called Gabriel, he not only told him that Samuel was going to be his new best man, but he also told Gabriel he was no longer invited to the wedding. Gabriel could not believe that his only brother would treat him like that.

"I've been home many times, but you're never there. Where are you now?"

"I'm out of town for a few weeks," Gabriel replied.

At that moment, Laurie realized that Gabriel came to Michigan not to visit the city, but because there was something wrong between him and his brother. She had doubted, but now she became certain that Gabriel never told his brother about his visits with her.

The gentleman did not dare to ask his brother about his new location. He said, "All right, so... I want to talk to you about my future since you're the only family I have."

"I'm listening."

"It seemed I was too emotional on my decision. I didn't think enough," the gentleman acknowledged.

"What happened?"

"I feel like I'm in jail and the only time I'm happy is when I'm out. I don't think me and Barbara are compatible."

"What do you mean?" Gabriel asked his brother as he maintained his voice even.

"We don't play together. I can't joke around with her. She's always serious and only talking about the marriage. She doesn't care about my family. Can you believe that? We've been living together for three weeks and she never, never asked me about our parents," the gentleman complained.

"Wow... I feel you man, but my question is, does any woman ever fit in your life or is compatible with you?"

Gabriel paused and then continued, "Let's be honest, you always bring that same compatibility concern every time you have to take a step forward with someone. You may love someone, but you never fight to keep that person. Did you ever evaluate yourself? I know for sure, you are a good man. I'm proud of you as a brother. However, you're a dictator. You set so many rules for anyone who wants to become part of your life. You always want people to learn from you, but you never tried to learn from anybody. You want people to listen to you, and you barely listen to them. You never give someone a second chance. You project a selfish image of your personality. Trust me, ain't easy for someone to live with you, and I know you better than anybody else."

"You're right Gabe."

For an instant, Gabriel thought his brother hung up because he heard nothing else from him. He was about to press the end call button when the gentleman said, "However, I've met the woman of my heart."

"What happened with her and who was that lucky one?" Gabriel mocked in a joking way.

"I let her go. I've tried to find her everywhere in the city, but I can't. They said she was fired at her job and it seems like she left New York. I really don't know what I should do to see her again, at least to apologize to her."

"You still didn't say her name," Gabriel said.

"Is it a confession session? You're a priest now?" the gentleman mocked.

"Her name?" Gabriel insisted.

Laurie thought the gentleman was about to pronounce the name of his ex, Angela Braz. The one for whom he was carrying the dog tag around his neck. Laurie's heart started pounding like she was one of the contestants in a room waiting for her name to be called as the winner even though she felt she would barely make third place. Her relationship with the gentleman did not even last two months. Even Gabriel was impatiently waiting to know the name of the only one woman who had ever reached the deepest part of his brother's heart.

"The wolverine lady," the gentleman answered.

When Laurie heard the gentleman say the wolverine lady, she was shocked. If she'd followed her instincts, she would have screamed and jumped up and down to express her happiness and excitement. However, she put her right hand over her mouth as her eyes filled with tears of joy.

Gabriel laughed. He wanted to say something to his brother about the wolverine lady, but he promised Laurie to keep it a secret. He said, "Oh man!"

"In three days, I will marry a stranger. I know that I have to open myself up and try to get to know Barbara as you said. I hope it will work. It's gonna be hard because my heart is dedicated to the wolverine lady after all."

"Do you remember how you always advise your friends to listen to their hearts when it comes to love?" Gabriel asked.

"Yup, I do... By the way, I actually want to see you at the wedding. I would be more than happy to have your presence. The ceremony will take place at St Peter's church on 86th Street, in Manhattan, on Saturday at 11:00 o'clock. And we will go together to the party. I'll text you the address."

"We'll see," Gabriel said.

"All right. Take care man," the gentleman said before he hung up the phone.

Once the gentleman hung up, Laurie stepped out on her tiptoes, and sat down on the wooden stairs in front of the entrance door. She looked at the sky and closed her eyes as a soft breeze caressed the trees. For the first time since that Friday night when she slept with the gentleman, she found peace for her soul. Although she was not the bride, she was relieved at the thought of knowing she was the one the gentleman truly loved.

Carlette came back from grocery shopping. Laurie walked back inside with her mother and pretended she knew nothing about the recent conversation between Gabriel and the gentleman. Gabriel was already dressed when Carlette returned. So he went to the car and helped them carry the rest groceries inside, Carlette and Laurie unpacked the bags and put the items away.

Laurie was so happy that she cooked diner. Hearing the gentleman's voice on the phone and knowing he loved her gave Laurie strength and energy.

Following the first taste, Gabriel stared at Laurie. She looked back at him as she smiled and snapped, "What?"

I Dare You To Try It

Gabriel remained silent for a few seconds and answered her with a question as he glanced at Laurie and then Carlette, "Is it a family thing?"

"What are you talking about?" Laurie asked in confusion.

"The cooking. I thought it was only your mother, but I was totally wrong," Gabriel replied.

"Oh… You like it?"

He nodded, "Yes, I do." He took another bite and said, "It's delicious."

"I can teach you if you want," Laurie offered.

"When will we start?"

"What you're eating now is a pork loin with sauerkraut and mashed potatoes."

Laurie gave him additional information about that specialty. After dinner, they watched a movie before they went to sleep.

Around 2:15 a.m., Carlette was going to the kitchen to get water when she heard Gabriel say, "Come onnnn…." At first, she thought he was on the phone. To her big surprise she heard her daughter laughing and said, "That's enough. Good night." Gabriel replied with delight, "Nite, nite…"

Carlette remained quiet in the dark kitchen and watched Laurie leave Gabriel's room with a big smile on her face. The most intriguing thing for Carlette was the way her daughter walked on her tip toes to not make any noise with her feet. Carlette could have called Laurie and asked her what she was doing with Gabriel, but her daughter was no longer a child or a teenager.

Carlette became confused. She was disturbed by some unanswered questions: What was her daughter doing that late with Gabriel in his room? Why had Gabriel come to spend so many days in Michigan while he used to stay for just one night before he went back to New York? Why had Gabriel mentioned nothing about his brother during his long stay? Carlette thought she would have been back home before Laurie came back from her clinic visit. However it was the opposite. Why had Laurie looked so happy all of a sudden and even cooked dinner? Carlette was asking herself if she missed the big picture. She found bizarre the fact that Laurie stopped talking about the gentleman, but instead was praising Gabriel's demeanor.

In the morning, it was even more difficult for Carlette as she was observing her daughter's new attitude. When Laurie woke up, she went to Gabriel's room, woke him up, and cooked him breakfast. Carlette wanted to ask Anna's advice about this; however, she did not want to tarnish her daughter's reputation that was already at stake. Carlette could not believe that so many things had happened once she retired. She went to New York in May to celebrate her retirement, and since then troubles had not stopped coming into her family. She was aware that it would be sad for her to live as a widower, but she never expected that she would have to deal with so many problems. Carlette felt like she was on an emotional rollercoaster. She realized the best thing she could do was to hold on tight until the ride was over, even though she had no clue how long the ride would last.

SEPTEMBER 28, 2012

The day before the wedding, early in the morning, the gentleman was watching the news and saw a report about thieves in bars and nightclubs. The reporter explained how some scammers partnered with bartenders to steal people's money in these places. These thieves-bartenders swiped the debit or credit cards twice in two different machines: one swipe for the bar and another swipe to empty the card. Those bartenders received forty percent of any deal made during one night. To make the money untraceable, the scammers used gift cards to redistribute the money because it was difficult for any federal agency to trace the origin of the money. The reporter said over three million dollars were stolen in less than four months in New York and Miami alone.

One FBI agent interviewed by the reporter, acknowledged that those scammers used a big network for their transactions. He stated the FBI was working hard to find the source and arrest those people. The agent also stated that the scammers struck at the perfect time: summer. Everybody was out for fun and having a good time. Their victims were those customers who told bartenders to keep their cards open. The majority of the victims became aware of their loss two or three weeks later because they had many credit cards. The card they used in one night was used again maybe two to three weeks later.

This propelled the gentleman to check his bank account to see if everything was correct because he and Barbara went out eight days ago. For curiosity and precaution, he did not simply verify the activity of his account for last week, but he did for the entire month. He reviewed all the transactions made on his account. For every check, he looked on the Internet to verify the address if the beneficiaries were companies.

The gentleman was surprised to see how his fiancé was spending his money on jewelry and in the past two weeks, Barbara bought some expensive stuff for the new apartment she moved into with her fiancé on Chelsea Piers. She was throwing money out the window. Obviously it was not her money, and she did not work for it. So she was careless about it.

The gentleman could not complain too much. Barbara was making ninety-five thousand a year without bonuses and driving an Audi A5 Cabriolet when he met her. Unlike Gabriel who made withdrawals on the account, the gentleman was able to see where and how his fiancé spent his money. He knew that he would have to talk to Barbara otherwise he would have to file for bankruptcy in less than a year.

The gentleman saw three checks in the amount of sixty thousand dollars made on the name of the same doctor, Dr. Jose Bowman, Barbara's gynecologist. He found these expenses odd, and he wondered why Barbara had written those checks.

Around 10:15 a.m., the gentleman went to the doctor's clinic and asked him about the services he provided for such an amount of money. The doctor refused to cooperate and stated that it was his duty to protect his patients' information. After a long conversation, the gentleman proposed to the doctor to triple the money if the doctor told him the truth. The doctor accepted the offer and told the gentleman what he needed to hear. The gentleman secretly recorded the conversation on his phone while the doctor explained the service he provided to Barbara.

When Barbara woke up that morning, she saw a note from her fiancé on her pillow saying that he went out for a haircut. She took a shower, went to the kitchen, and ate her favorite breakfast: a yogurt, one green apple, and some strawberries.

Around 12:30 p.m., Barbara called every bridesmaid, every groomsman, the maid of honor, the priest, and the catering company for the party to make sure that everything was going according to her plan. Then, she packed her clothes for her honeymoon trip to Paris. She had booked the five-star *Hotel de l'Amour*. The gentleman had already packed his bag on Thursday.

Two hours later, Barbara left her apartment to finalize the wedding and honeymoon plans. She even bought herself a wedding gift: an Audi R8 fully loaded in cash, but she agreed with the dealer to pick it up after the honeymoon. She had a 4:00 p.m. appointment at the salon for a massage, facial, and nails.

The gentleman called her and told her she would not see him the day prior to the wedding because it was bad luck. He also told her Samuel planned a bachelor party for him so he would be with his cousin for the rest of the day.

Barbara was more than happy with the plans of her fiancé, but she made him swear to be on time at the church. Barbara was already dreaming about her crown following her successful victories. Meanwhile, she was impatiently waiting to enjoy her bachelorette party and the last night she would be single.

Around 8:30 p.m., Perez was already waiting for the gentleman at *Sweet'S* on 12th avenue and 65th Street in Manhattan. When Perez walked in and glanced around. He saw many young people, who appeared to be college students, sitting around tables and smoking hookah. Perez could not believe that the gentleman would celebrate his bachelor party in such a boring place. The place looked more like a place for students to come and chill, not what he expected for a bachelor party.

As Perez was waiting for the gentleman, he walked to the bar and asked for a beer. To his surprise, the bartender told him they did not have a permit for alcohol. Perez thought this was some kind of joke and wondered why his colleague chose this place. Fifteen minutes later, Perez saw the gentleman walking towards him with two men. He thought those two men were the gentleman's bodyguards.

"What's up bro?" the gentleman asked as he shook Perez's hand.

"Nothing much moneyman, just chilling," Perez replied.

"This is my cousin Samuel, and his friend Jonathan," the gentleman said.

"Nice to meet you guys," Perez greeted them as he shook their hands.

"Do you like the place?" Samuel asked Perez.

"Are you kidding me right now? This place is for kids. Can't you see? It's dead. We don't need to be so dressed up for this place. Fellas, let's get out of here. Let's go to *Heaven* and show this gentleman a good time," Perez said.

"I feel you... But this was Sam's idea," the gentleman added.

Perez gave a shocked look to the gentleman to show how disappointed he was about the place. He threw his hands in exasperation and called out, "Come on, man..."

Perez continued, "Why didn't you let me take care of this? Samuel ain't know shit." Perez glanced at the best man and apologized. "No disrespect man."

"It's aright man," Samuel replied as he stood up and said, "I'll be right back. I'm going to the bar."

"Get me a smoothie," Perez said to Samuel in a mocking tone.

Samuel smiled at Perez and headed to the bar. When he arrived at the bar, he showed the bartender a text message that contained a code. She confirmed the code and gave Samuel four cards.

Perez asked the gentleman, "So we gonna spend the night here? Getting high with this hookah shit."

The gentleman shrugged. "I guess…"

"Sweet…" Perez mocked.

Two minutes later, Samuel came back and asked them to follow him. They walked toward the entrance door then opened the second set of doors to leave the place. Samuel gave four tickets to a bouncer who stood in front of a door stamped with a big S. Once the bouncer finished checking them, he opened the door and let them through.

Perez, Jonathan, and the gentleman followed Samuel into a long hallway with faint lights. At the end of the hallway, Samuel opened a door on his right and then they took the stairs to a basement. Only Samuel was not freaked out by the place because he had been there before with his boss many times. Once they reached the basement, there was a door in front of them with a flashing sign of *Sweet'S*.

I Dare You To Try It

When they walked in, they heard the music playing, and a pretty lady wearing only a shiny silver thong bikini, greeted them, "Welcome to *Sweet'S*." Samuel gave her the card he received from the bartender in the hookah place upstairs. She asked them to follow her. Besides the light set up and the waitresses, nothing looked exciting inside. It seemed like *Sweet'S* was empty with about twenty men sitting at the bar. The place looked like more than a sports bar than a strip club.

Perez was already staring at the waitress's behind as she led them to a room. He nudged the gentleman and nodded. The waitress stopped in front of room number 10 and said, "Here is your suite. Have fun."

Samuel thanked the waitress and said to the gentleman, "This is your bachelor party. Come and open your bachelor gift."

The gentleman smiled, walked, and opened the door. Before, he could even say a word, Perez called out, "Ohh… shiiiiitttttt!!!!" before he jumped on Samuel and said, "That's what I'm talking about bro!!!"

Perez, Jonathan, Samuel, and the gentleman walked in the room and shut the door behind them. They were standing in a big room and looking at eight strippers that Samuel ordered. These women were crazy beautiful. The room had four red leather sofas, two poles for the strippers, and one bottle of champagne with two glasses next to each sofa.

"Boys, stay alive," Samuel said as looked at Perez and patted his left shoulder. Within a few seconds the strippers were already grinding their ass on the four men to the sound of the music. It did not take long for Perez to start grabbing the strippers' asses.

Fifteen minutes later, the gentleman walked out of the room and came back with forty thousand dollars in twenty-dollar bill rolls. He gave three rolls of two thousand to each of the three guys and kept the rest.

Sweet'S was opened two days a week: Friday and Saturday. It had ten rooms, each one with a security guard. Reservations for a room had to be made at least one month in advance. But they made an exception when it came to the gentleman because he was famous. Samuel's boss also helped out in securing the room. Each room was fifteen hundred dollars flat for two hours; each stripper cost one thousand dollars per hour. For every five thousand spent, the customer received one bottle of his choice. No more than five customers were allowed in a room.

Everything was allowed in the room besides sex and any recording devices. Some faithful and trusted customers could even buy cocaine. Only a trusted customer could get a pass for another friend. *Sweet'S* was owned by an Albanian mafia; no one dared to mess with them. They were so powerful and had such a big network that they ran a security check on every single customer including the faithful and trusted ones. Following each reservation, a security code was sent to get cards at the front door.

After the first thirty minutes, strippers were dancing naked, and the floor of the room was changed into twenty-dollar bills. Samuel saw that his cousin was not enjoying the party. So he asked the gentleman, "What's wrong with you?"

The gentleman looked at his cousin, nodded, and replied, "I'm alright," as he tried to manage a fake smile to reassure Samuel.

Perez added, "He's getting locked up tomorrow. That's why." He paused and then advised the gentleman, "If I were you I would enjoy my last day of freedom."

Twenty minutes later, the gentleman said, "Guys, I'm gonna leave you. Gotta go somewhere else - it's important."

"What are you talking about? You agreed when I told you I booked the place for three hours. We just spent fifty minutes and you're already leaving?" Samuel asked with a confused face.

"No you stay guys. I'll take a cab. Can't miss it…" the gentleman insisted.

Jonathan remained quiet. Samuel was not happy with his cousin's decision. Perez patted the gentleman on the back and said, "I got you… The man has a special date. Go man. Hit that pussy hard," as he laughed out loud.

The gentleman slapped every single stripper's ass, then he gave another four thousand dollars to each of his guests, and said, "See y'all tomorrow." He also tipped the bouncer who was in the room and the waitress who welcomed them at the door. It was 9:50 p.m., when he left the club, took a taxi, and went to an unknown destination.

Meanwhile, Barbara and her friends were partying hard at *Caliente,* a nightclub with male and female strippers. *Caliente* was a nightclub popular for bachelor and bachelorette parties.

Under Laurie's insistence, Gabriel went back to New York to witness the marriage of his one and only brother. She helped him choose his suit and tie for the wedding. It was 10:45 p.m. when he got home. Gabriel called Laurie to tell her he arrived home safely. Laurie thought Gabriel could be hungry, so she ordered pizza online for him. Gabriel was surprised when someone knocked at his door to deliver the pizza. Laurie told him it came from her. They spent almost two hours on the phone before Gabriel went to sleep.

Laurie realized that she did not fight at all to keep her lover. So she tried to make desperate moves. The idea of contacting Gabriel and the way she treated him were not a coincidence. Based on the way the gentleman described his relationship with his little brother, Laurie had an intuition that Gabriel could help her rectify the situation.

That morning when Carlette saw her daughter laughing and coming out of Gabriel's room was nothing special. Laurie went downstairs to get water and saw the light in Gabriel's room was on. So, she checked on him. Carlette came downstairs five minutes later and thought her daughter had been with Gabriel in his room for a while.

The choice of Gabriel's suit, the pizza, and the long hours on the phone were aimed to play on Gabriel's mind and raise his sensitivity and compassion. Laurie convinced Gabriel to go to the wedding because she believed somehow that he would oppose to the marriage between Barbara and the gentleman.

SATURDAY, SEPTEMBER 29, 2012

Around 4:00 a.m., Laurie heard a creak from the door of her room. She saw the door open; a man closed it behind him and walked slowly towards her in the dark. The silence of the night terrified her. At first, she thought Barbara sent a criminal after her. Laurie quickly sat up in her bed and held her pillow tight against her chest. She was scared to death and out of breath. She wanted to scream, but for an unknown reason, she did not. The closer the man got, the louder her heart pounded.

A couple of feet closer and away from the shadow, Laurie saw the gentleman's face. She sighed, climbed off her bed, and jumped in his arms. She held the gentleman and wrapped her arms around his waist. And then she raised her chin to look at him and ask him some questions such as:

What was he doing in Michigan? How did he get there? What's going on with the wedding?

As Laurie opened her mouth to question him, the gentleman put his right index finger on her lips, shushed her, and took her in his embrace. Laurie looked at him once again, right before she even said a word, and the gentleman kissed her and squeezed the flesh of her ass. He edged away from her a little, and then he took off her nightdress and his clothes. He put her on her bed and continued to kiss her.

After caressing her for a few minutes, the gentleman positioned Laurie's legs like the letter V and his legs made an upside down V. He slid his arms into her legs, grabbed her shoulders, and then he started his in and out moves with his waist. Laurie moaned — the pleasure was intense. She grasped her bed because she did not want to scratch his back again like she did the first time.

The gentleman switched to another position. He made a rectangular triangle with her legs. His right hand kept pressing her left leg on the bed; he folded her right leg and held them under his left shoulder to maintain the perfect ninety-degree angle. And then, he extended his left arm until he reached her breast and rolled the mound of her right nipple with his index finger and thumb.

The gentleman knew how to provide her with sweet pleasure. Her breasts were her weak spot. He sped up and her adrenaline rose. Laurie continued to moan. She was close to having an orgasm. Suddenly, her mother knocked at her door and asked, "Laurie, are you okay?" Carlette knocked again and again, and kept asking the same question since she did not receive any response. Unfortunately, her daughter could not answer her due to the pleasure she felt. The sound that resonated outside Laurie's room was like she was crying, but a sweet cry. But for Laurie, her moan was like a volcano that was about to erupt.

Since Carlette did not receive any answer, she opened the door, and turned on the light. Her daughter did not expect at all that her mother would interrupt her pleasure like that.

"Yes, mom, I am fine," Laurie snapped in the sweaty sheets of her bed.

Carlette pressed her lips, glared at her daughter for almost two minutes without saying a word. Then she shook her head, turned off the light, and went back to her room.

Laurie wished she had locked her door. Her mother would never interrupt her ascending to the seventh heaven. That dream was so vivid and carried such an undeniable pleasure that she was still breathing heavily after Carlette left. Laurie put one pillow between her legs and hugged another pillow. She wished so bad to hold the gentleman in her arms and smell his cologne.

Laurie was trembling. The worst part was that her mother disturbed her when she was just about to orgasm. She could not sleep anymore; her temperature rose, and she felt some kind of heartache due to her longing for the gentleman. She became aggravated, annoyed, and frustrated.

A few minutes later, Laurie went to the bathroom, opened the shower, and let ice-cold water pour down her body. She folded her arms and held her forearms with her hands. The tears falling down her cheeks explained her desolation. The gentleman was about to be married in a couple of hours to a woman who was once her best friend. Laurie realized that the gentleman would only be hers in her dreams with the hope that nobody would come to disturb her.

Two hours later, Laurie was still in the bathroom. Carlette entered and saw her daughter shaking in the ice-cold water. Carlette took a towel, turned off the water, and wrapped Laurie. Carlette took her daughter to her room as she tried to dry her. Once she got into the room, she stripped off her daughter's wet clothes, and went to a closet. Carlette grabbed a comforter and cover Laurie with it. And then, she made tea with cinnamon and ginger to warm up Laurie's body. A few minutes later, Carlette made Laurie some soup.

As a woman, Carlette understood the pain that her daughter had to endure. She wished to give her daughter a speech of comfort. Unfortunately, her brain was frozen. The absence of the gentleman affected Carlette as well. She remained silent during all the time she was providing care to her daughter.

Laurie had been in denial; when the wedding day finally came, it was a complete desolation for her. It was like someone precious to her was dying. As her mother was rubbing her back, Laurie fell asleep and her river of tears stopped.

As planned, the wedding day was respected. All guests gathered to celebrate the joyful love of the future couple. Some were talking in subdued tones and others were taking photos with their phones. Everyone was on time and looked gorgeous. The media came out to cover the event.

As soon as the gentleman walked into the church, he saw his brother. He was more than happy to see Gabriel. He ran and hugged him. The gentleman felt that his little brother's presence was like an angel sent from heaven. The gentleman took his brother in a corner and whispered to him before he gave Gabriel a cellphone.

Three white limousines were parked in front of St Peter's Church. The first one with Barbara's family members, the second one transported the five bridesmaids and groomsmen, the flower girl, and the ring boy. The maid of honor and the bride were sitting in the third one. The procession made its entry according to the order of the limos and accompanied by a pianist who played a symphony of love.

The bridesmaids were dressed in light pink and held a bouquet made of twenty-four roses mixed with white and red roses in equal proportion. The girls were so beautiful and sexy that they looked like angels from heaven. Each of their smiles was like a unique firework.

Any magazine could have hired the groomsmen. They looked like models in their black tuxedos, light pink shirts, and black bowties with a boutonniere on the left side of their chest. They were all handsome and some single ladies present at the church were already thinking about their moves to catch those groomsmen's attention.

The gentleman and Samuel were standing at the altar and waiting for Barbara. Once they announced the coming of the bride, everyone present stood and clapped their hands to salute her. The pianist started playing the wedding song. The bride wore a white mermaid wedding dress. Half way through, the gentleman who was forcing a smile walked toward Barbara. He took her right hand and brought her in front of the priest to the altar. She carried a bouquet of forty-eight roses in front of her.

Once everything was in place, the priest started the ceremony by saying, "We are gathered on this beautiful morning to witness the exchange of vows of an everlasting love..."

Barbara spent a lot of money on that wedding. The decorations came out wonderfully, and the bridesmaids and groomsmen looked gorgeous. So far, everything was going according to her plan. Flashes from cameras were coming from all directions. Some women whispered that they found it strange the fact that Barbara was still so petite with no fullness on her belly since they knew she was pregnant.

The priest continued the ceremony. When he reached one of the most important parts of the ceremony, he glanced respectively at Barbara and the gentleman and said, "The vows you are about to exchange will serve as a verbal representation of the non-verbal emotions that are as real as anything that can be seen, heard, or touched. Does anyone here know something that could stop this beautiful couple from being united?"

Barbara turned her head to see if there was anyone who would oppose to her wedding. Suddenly Gabriel stood up, Barbara got nervous and she could hear her heart pounding. She asked herself, *how the hell did this asshole get there?* She thought Gabriel was about to say something and oppose. However, he walked toward the back of the church where they maintained the sound's equipment. She sighed and turned back toward the priest.

The priest continued the ceremony and said, "Since there is no objection and you comply with the laws regarding marriage in the State of New York, I will proceed to your union. At this time, I will ask you to face each other and take each other's hands."

The priest paused as he was waiting for the couple to do what he asked them, then he looked at the gentleman, and asked, "Do you take Barbara Babino as your spouse, to cherish her, and to live together with her in the covenant of marriage? Do you promise to love her, to comfort her, to honor her, and to keep her in sickness and health, and forsaking all others? Be faithful to her as you both shall live?"

"No, I don't," the gentleman replied with a firm tone of voice.

"What?" everyone in the church exclaimed including Barbara.

"Can you repeat that?" the priest asked to make sure of the gentleman's decision.

"I'm sorry. I can't marry her. I want to be with somebody else," the groom answered.

"Who's that?" Barbara asked in fury.

"Laurie."

"Are you leaving me for that bitch?"

"Yes I am. At least she's true to me."

"But I love you and you swore to marry me after I lost our child because of your brother."

"No, no honey, let's get it straight... you love my money not me. Oh! By the way, I talked to the doctor, your gynecologist. He told me everything," the gentleman said.

"That's bullshit. You're a liar," Barbara retorted.

"Oh yeah... Let's listen to this tape together. Gabe, go ahead. Play it."

Gabriel played the tape on the speaker. And everybody heard, "Barbara Babino has been my patient for approximately six years. I'm her gynecologist. She was seen in my office five months ago with her ex-fiancé for blood tests to make sure they could conceive. We found some irregularities with her. I suggested further tests regarding the matter. She was supposed to come back to the clinic for the results, but she cancelled her appointment and told us she was going away for her job. Before her engagement with you, she came to the clinic, and I told her she's infertile. I was surprised to hear the news that she was pregnant with your child. Two weeks later, she came back and bribed me with a check of sixty thousand dollars to write a letter for her that stated she had a miscarriage. I didn't want to do that, but she insisted and tripled the offer and gave me evidence she had been pregnant. So I accepted the offer to create a file for her and gave her the letter. I prescribed her some medications, but it was only vitamins. She told me she had to do that, otherwise she would lose a fortune."

Barbara cleared her throat and looked around. The maid of honor shrugged in disbelief. Everyone present at the wedding was shocked and gaped at the couple when the gentleman called off the wedding. They could not believe that Barbara was that greedy. The guests started whispering. Definitely, the gentleman was always in the spotlight since the shooting.

Barbara pointed her index finger toward Gabriel and said, "You made that up." She continued to defend herself;

she looked at her fiancé, and said, "Honey, this is a plot by your brother because he doesn't want us to be together. Do you remember what he did with your money and how he tried to kill me?"

"That's true. I don't want my brother to be with an evil person like you," Gabriel said.

Barbara became frustrated, pushed her fiancé, threw her bouquet in Gabriel's face, and said, "You've ruined my life."

The gentleman could no longer wait to put an end to the relationship with Barbara. He was ready to pay any price to be freed from her. He could have cancelled the wedding without being at the church. Since his relationship with Barbara started with big media coverage, he also wanted it to end the same way. The gentleman glanced at his fiancé and said, "You can take everything you want. It's over between us,"

Gabriel left the church with his brother followed by Samuel. When they got into the car, the gentleman said that he needed to leave the city for a couple of weeks because it would be too crazy for him with the media. Gabriel advised him to go to Michigan to explore. The gentleman agreed to his little brother's idea and Samuel drove them to the airport.

While on the plane, Gabriel told his brother the truth about his faked film training in upstate New York. Once landed, they took a taxi and went to Carlette's house. Gabriel called Laurie and asked her to come and open the door because he was back from the wedding. However, he mentioned nothing about the wedding cancellation and the presence of his brother with him.

Laurie came and opened the door. She was shocked to see Gabriel and the gentleman standing outside. She glanced at Gabriel, shook her head, and said, "You betrayed me Gabe."

"I know and I'm sorry. But the child will need his father," Gabriel pleaded.

"Can the child trust either you?" Laurie asked as she glanced at each one of the brothers.

While Laurie and Gabriel were exchanging words, the gentleman was admiring the wolverine lady. He felt like years had passed since he'd seen her. Finally, he stepped out of his silent box and mumbled, "Mmm… Laurie."

Before he could even finish his sentence, Laurie pointed out her index finger and snapped, "Don't say a word. I'm not talking to you yet."

Laurie's demeanor was unexpected by both brothers. For a moment Gabriel could not believe her reaction.

"I kept it a secret, but I know that you both miss each other. And I don't want to travel in secret every single time I want to see you and my nephew or niece."

"Nobody forces you to travel. You know what? I don't wanna see you anymore," Laurie replied as she referred to both brothers.

Carlette was in her room when she looked out the window and saw Gabriel and the gentleman standing in front of the house with Laurie. She ran downstairs and opened the door. However, she stopped as soon as she opened the door because the scene told her that there was tension between the three. Since she did not know how it started, she remained silent and watched the show.

"Please don't blame Gabe. Put the blame on me. I deserve it. I'm deeply sorry for what I've caused in your life. I understand you may not allow me to come and see our child, but please let my brother come. At least our child will see his uncle. I also want you to know that I always love you," the gentleman said in a soft voice.

"Wow... Really... you love me?" Laurie paused, stared at the gentleman, and then asked, "How can you love me when you just got married to another woman?"

"Last time I checked, single men wear tuxedos too," the gentleman answered with a smile and showed her his fingers.

Laurie looked at Gabriel who told her that the wedding did not happen. She continued, "Do you have any idea how people feel about you?"

"Please forgive me. I am here for you," the gentleman begged.

"Is it some kind of a joke or a game? You slept with her then pretended to love me. You threw me away like trash and got engaged to her. You dumped her on your wedding day and then say you want me back. I don't wanna be involved in that back and forth crap anymore."

The gentleman would have never thought Laurie would be so harsh to him like that. He felt she would not forgive him. For a moment, she pretended to be resolute but deep inside she could not wait to be in his embrace for real. She was more than happy that the wedding did not happen.

Laurie glared at the gentleman for a few seconds as she replayed all the good moments she had with him: their encounter, their first kiss, his funny jokes, the sweet night they shared, and the way he saved her.

"I apologized for my mistakes Laurie. You are the one I want. The only one I really love. Trust me. I mean it."

"I think you are meant to be together, especially when he discovered the truth about Barbara. I think you both should give a chance to your future, guys. You love each other. He's my brother and you're already part of this family. I want you for my brother," Gabriel stated.

"You saved my life," Laurie acknowledged.

"You resurrected my heart," the gentleman said.

Laurie sighed and stared at the gentleman for a few seconds. She realized that he could have blamed her for not visiting him even once at the hospital and for calling him a — *poor bouncer,* but instead he was begging for her forgiveness. She released her divine smile and confessed, "Your courage gains my heart. Thank you for saving my life. In your presence I forget all my bad memories. How could I not love you when your kindness and caring go beyond measure?"

Anna was running to break the news to Carlette about the wedding between Barbara and the gentleman, when she saw Laurie kissing him. Carlette was more than happy for her daughter especially to see her back with the gentleman. Anna ran, hugged the gentleman and Laurie, and said, "I'm so proud of you both. The prophecy is accomplished. Oh boy! You still carry that smell. Laurie, you better tell him to not hug any other women. Otherwise, you'll be in trouble."

They all laughed out loud and then walked inside the house. The gentleman explained to Laurie and her mother how he discovered the truth about Barbara who faked her pregnancy.

Barbara knew there was no way she could be pregnant unless it was a miracle. She went to a public hospital in Brooklyn and paid five thousand dollars in cash to a pregnant woman in exchange for her urine. She was also eating a lot of fast food and drinking soda, so that her belly could look bloated. When Barbara's gynecologist requested a release of her information from the public hospital, they faxed him her records, so he could complete her file at the clinic. Barbara almost succeeded with her plan.

There was a basketball game that was about to start. The gentleman tried to order pizzas, but his debit card was denied. At first sight, he thought he entered wrong numbers. He reviewed everything and processed the transaction one more time. However, the result was the same. Therefore, he checked his account on his cellphone. Then, he started laughing and shaking his head.

Laurie asked him if he was okay, but he could not say a word. Laurie panicked and asked him, "What's wrong with you?"

"I only have forty-six cents in my account now. Barbara withdrew all the money," the gentleman replied.

"How's that possible?" Laurie asked.

"I gave her access to my account."

"When did she withdraw the money?" Anna asked.

"This afternoon."

"You should call the police. That bitch is a thief," Laurie advised.

"I can't call the police. When I was leaving the church I told her to take everything she wanted."

The gentleman took a deep breath and put his hands on his face. He was thinking about how he would take care of his family. Laurie lost her job, and his brother just finished school. Barbara hurt him badly. One should never undertake a relationship with someone without a heartfelt connection, because in the end, one will feel disgust. That news sank everyone into despair.

One minute later, Gabriel said, "Take this card bro."

"No man. Don't worry I will find a way to take care of her and my child," the gentleman said.

"Do you remember the saving account we opened together three years ago?" Gabriel asked.

"Yeah. I thought that account was closed," the gentleman replied.

"Nope. Check it out. Same password."

"Don't worry Gabe. We'll find a solution. Take care of your school bills. I will try to find another job here. If I can't, I will call Marc-Allan."

Gabriel insisted and his brother took the card. Laurie looked at both brothers without having any idea about the amount that was on the card. The gentleman checked the account on Gabriel's cellphone and said,

"Damn bro, you've been doing pretty well in saving. You've been making money in secret and you never told me about it."

"No man. That $654,960 you see is your money. When I knew Laurie was pregnant I withdrew money every day from your checking account. I had a feeling that Barbara wouldn't let you take care of Laurie and the child. Only 60 dollars is mine, all the rest is yours."

Laurie screamed loud and exclaimed, "Oh my gosh!" Then, she shed tears of joy.

The gentleman jumped on his brother, hugged him, and stated, "You're the best, bro."

"Thanks man, and remember that I'll always love you," Gabriel stated.

Laurie, Gabriel, and the gentleman had a big family hug. Anna and Carlette were speechless. The only thing they could do was clap their hands like they did when Laurie and the gentleman kissed in front of *The Flow*. Anna and Carlette shed tears of joy. They were so happy to see Laurie and the bouncer reunited. The gentleman ordered pizzas and entertained everyone with Joe's jokes.

Carlette was a big fan of wine. She brought two bottles of French wine into the living room. It was a wonderful night for a great celebration. That night, Laurie sipped cranberry juice and shed tears because she could not believe that meeting with the bouncer could have changed her life forever.

As they were watching the game, the gentleman saw a commercial about a cruise ship. He proposed to everyone to go with him on a trip to visit some Caribbean islands. They all agreed because they thought it could be a fun and relaxing vacation. In addition, it would be great to see different things from different environments. The next morning, he told Gabriel about his plan for that trip.

OCTOBER 10, 2012

Anna, Carlette, Laurie, Gabriel, and the gentleman took a plane to Miami where they boarded a cruise ship for seven days. As soon as Laurie and the gentleman boarded, people recognized them. However, it was different because those people had their mind set on vacation. Even though many people wanted to take pictures with the gentleman, they allowed privacy to the couple. Some people whispered about Laurie next to him. The next day, early in the morning, the cruise stopped in the Bahamas. It was their first trip to a Caribbean island. They had a wonderful time playing with dolphins and going on excursions on motorcycles.

The next destination was Labadee Hispaniola, a peninsula on the northern coast of Haiti with clean, warm, and beautiful beaches. Around noon, the passengers landed in Labadee Hispaniola. They could not believe such a beautiful place existed in Haiti, especially after the earthquake that devastated the country in January 2010. When Anna asked a bartender if the place was newly built, he told her that Labadee has been there for years and many cruises have stopped by. He told her that they tell the passengers this piece of land was called *Paradise Island* and they never mentioned it was part of Haiti.

After exploring the shores for a few minutes, they split and did their own activity. Gabriel was taking pictures as usual. Anna and Carlette were getting massages at the spa, and Laurie was sitting on a beach chair, sipping fresh coconut water that came straight from the trees, and watching men, including the gentleman, play beach volleyball. She wore a strapless navy knee length summer dress with gold flip-flops and a beige sun hat.

In the meantime, there was a sexy blonde lady lying on an inclined beach bed with black sunglasses. She was sipping a margarita as she was getting tanned. She had a curvy body and wore a white string bikini. With a disinterested look, she was also watching the men playing volleyball on the sand. With her sunglasses, nobody could tell what or who she was actually looking at. However, Laurie had an intuition that the blonde was eyeing the gentleman. Therefore, she kept an eye on the blonde. Laurie suspected something was up with that blonde and became angry because she was jealous.

Once the game was done, the gentleman stripped his white t-shirt off and went to swim. On his way back, the blonde walked toward him, put her hand on his chest and slid her hand down his muscular body. She said with a big smile in her face, "I know you. You're ..."

Before she even finished her sentence, Laurie snapped, "With me." Laurie grabbed the lady's hand off of the gentleman's chest and threw it away in fury. The blonde almost fell on the sand and understood that it would not be a good idea to approach the gentleman. Laurie opened her eyes wide to look at the lady like a tiger who was about to catch its prey. Afraid, the blonde walked away without saying anything.

The gentleman did not anticipate the moves of Laurie and the blonde. He glanced at Laurie, saw her facial expression, and understood that it was better for him to remain silent. He took her left hand and walked with her toward the bar. When they got to the bar, he ordered a *Prestige*, a Haitian beer. The gentleman told Laurie a joke about Joe and made her smile again.

Anna and Carlette came back from the spa and met Laurie and the gentleman at the bar. They waited ten minutes before Gabriel joined them. They were all hungry and were about to order food from the bar when the curvy blonde came and ordered food. Laurie asked Anna and Carlette to go and eat on the ship with her because she did not feel comfortable with the food that was served at the bar.

Gabriel said that he wanted to try every dish on the island. The gentleman wished to do the same as his brother, but he did not dare to stay following the incident that happened after the beach volleyball. He knew there was absolutely no way for Laurie to feel comfortable with him staying with Gabriel, especially with the blonde's presence at the bar. The gentleman and the three women went inside the boat.

After eating their food, they all went to their rooms for a nap. Two hours later, Gabriel came and asked his brother to go with him and try the Dragon's Breath zip line.

"It's too dangerous guys," Laurie said.

"No it's not, I bet if you were not pregnant you would try it," Gabriel teased.

"Nope, not me," she said.

"Let's go man. It's the longest zip line over water," Gabriel insisted.

The gentleman remained silent and watched Laurie and his brother talking about him like he was a child who needed permission from his parents to do something. Carlette came in the room to check on Laurie. She stopped at the door and listened to the conversation. The gentleman winked at her and she smiled at him.

"Gabe, your brother is not completely healed. Do you know that?" Laurie asked.

"It's not gonna do him any harm. It's a zip line, and it's gonna be fun," Gabriel pleaded.

I Dare You To Try It

"Okay I will go with you because there is nobody to stay with me," Laurie said when she realized that Gabriel would not give up on that project.

"I will stay with you. Let the boys have fun," Carlette said.

Laurie sighed and accepted to let her precious man go. The gentleman kissed her on the forehead and left the room with his brother. The biggest concern for Laurie was not the zip line, but the blonde. She saw how pretty and aggressive the blonde was.

"I understand how much you love him, but don't sound or act too possessive. Remember, they are not only brothers, but also best friends," Carlette advised her daughter.

One hour and half later, Gabriel came back without his brother. He told Laurie that the gentleman went to buy souvenirs. Thirty minutes passed and there was no sign of the gentleman. Laurie became more worried when she heard the sound of the ship's first horn. Anna advised them to split and go look for him otherwise he would be left behind. During the search, they heard the second horn. They panicked because the ship would leave the port after the third horn. They came back to the ship. There was a man with eyes facing the sea and dressed like a captain. Gabriel pointed him out and said to Laurie, "Go and talk to the captain at the bow to save the day."

"What am I gonna tell the captain? Your brother is not a child."

"Convince him to stay."

Laurie listened to Gabriel. However, instead of going at the bow, she went to the bridge of the ship to talk to the chief in command. Anna, Carlette, and Laurie ran inside the control room to explain the situation to the crew. The chief in command stated that he would not wait for any missing passenger and would stick to the cruise's rules.

"You can't leave him behind," Laurie argued.

"I am sorry Madame. If a passenger is not back on time, we have no choice. We need to respect our schedule. That was stated in black and white in the agreement form signed by each passenger," he replied with a French accent.

"I am not leaving without him," she yelled.

"I guess you could ask the other captain because I won't change my mind. We're sailing for our next destination, Madame."

Laurie left the control room and went to talk to the man dressed in white at the bow.

"Sir, can you please reason with the captain in the booth and tell him I am not leaving the father of my child behind. I won't lose him again."

The man in white turned around, kneeled in front of Laurie, and said, "Will you marry me?"

Besides Gabriel and the chief in command at the bridge, no one was aware of this proposal plan. In shock, she nodded and said, "Yes, yes I will" as tears of joy fell down her cheeks.

It was sunset and the cool breeze was felt, perfect scenery for a romantic moment. The gentleman put the ring on her finger and kissed her. Everybody present at that moment clapped their hands and took pictures of the couple.

Laurie and the gentleman got married two days later by a pastor in Aruba. They swore to stick together and be faithful to one another for the rest of their lives. It was a wonderful experience for them. Even though they did not have the luxury to see the entire cruise because so many people were asking the gentleman for photos, they enjoyed the weather and landscapes of the Caribbean islands.

Gabriel took a picture of Laurie and the gentleman after their wedding. That photo was all the buzz on social media. Laurie wore a navy blue three quarter sleeve sweater, white shorts with a brown belt, a long gold necklace, a chunky gold watch on her right hand, a chunky gold bracelet, brown flat sandals, and her wedding ring on her left hand. The gentleman wore a blue navy slim fit chino, a white short-sleeve shirt unbuttoned to the chest, a gold necklace around his neck, sunglasses, blue, red and white moccasins, and his wedding band.

Once landed in Miami, Gabriel went to New York. Carlette and Anna took a plane for Michigan. Laurie and the gentleman stayed in Miami for three days to shop before they went to Venice for their honeymoon. They spent seven days in Italy and visited Milan and Rome as well. They enjoyed their moment because it was peaceful and those cities were beautiful. No paparazzi harassed them.

EPILOGUE

On March 25, 2013, Laurie gave birth to a boy, Poborsky Junior. One month later, she opened an online marketing company that became very profitable and allowed her to take care of her family.

In August 2013, the gentleman, Geronimo Annastal, published his second book called *"Wanted Alive"*. That book was even more successful than the first one. It broke many records in book publishing history. He received many awards for *"Guilty of Natural Beauty."* There was no doubt he would also be nominated for the publication of his second book.

Geronimo became not only famous, but he was also an idol for many. His life story represented the vision of the United States of America, the only country in the world where anyone from any social class, any color, and any origin can make it to the top. His wife became his manager. Many companies endorsed him. He was in almost every single commercial on television.

Marvin Emmanuel Jerome, a film director in Hollywood, contacted the gentleman, and asked him to turn the second book into a movie. Geronimo welcomed the idea with delight; his manager signed the contract with Marvin. According to the film director, the movie would come out in autumn 2015.

September 2013, Gabriel Annastal built a photo and video studio on 55th Street, in Manhattan. He signed great contracts with different artists and models by using his brother's network. At the end of October 2013, Laurie and the gentleman moved to Los Angeles. Carlette moved with them as well.

The End

ABOUT THE AUTHOR

Elie Jerome is a young Haitian writer and poet who graduated with a Bachelor's degree from UNASMOH in Haiti in 2007 and a Master's degree in Emergency and Disaster Management in 2012 from Metropolitan College of New York.

Elie is a talented young man who is passionate about writing. In 2004 he began working on his own biography. After writing many unfinished stories, he decided to make his mark and publish his first book: *"I Dare You To Try It"*. He is currently working on his second novel: *"C'est La Vie (This Is Life)."* His stories are breathtaking, full of twists, and will blow the readers' minds.

Contact info:

eliejerome8@gmail.com

www.eliejerome1.com

Made in the USA
Charleston, SC
03 August 2016